Terror stalked a
dark forest road

With a jolt that almost knocked the wind out of her, Rosemary was seized by arms that crushed her like steel bands. A hand closed over her mouth and pulled her head back sharply.

Suddenly she knew that the men she'd been searching for—the gang of art thieves—had found *her* instead! Then her eyes widened in disbelief as she recognized the leader of the criminals striding toward her.

It was Thomas, her lifelong friend and the man she loved. But now he was a stranger to her—a stranger and a killer!

Other

MYSTIQUE BOOKS

by DENISE NOEL

For a free catalogue listing all available Mystique Books,
send your name and address to:

MYSTIQUE BOOKS,
M.P.O. Box 707, Niagara Falls, N.Y. 14302
In Canada: 649 Ontario St., Stratford, Ontario N5A 6W2

Death of a Stranger

by DENISE NOEL

MYSTIQUE BOOKS

TORONTO·LONDON·NEW YORK
HAMBURG·AMSTERDAM·STOCKHOLM

Chapter 1

Rosemary leaned out over the rocky chasm as far as she dared. For a dizzy moment she was numbed by fear. The sandstone cliff was steeper than she had thought. She clung to the slender trunk of a young poplar tree, trying to calculate the distance to the car, which lay twisted and crumpled on the rocks below. The bright red metal and glass caught the sun between the torn branches of the trees. It was only forty yards or so, but the drops were steep and sudden.

She could feel herself begin to perspire. Could she really make it down the rocky cliff? She *had* to make it. She must reach the wreckage and get the black attaché case from the trunk. And she had to do it quickly.

Pushing on the solid, rough surface beneath her feet, she swung out from the rock face and, stretching as far as she could before surrendering her handhold, jumped a deep fissure. The tree snapped back toward the sky. She grabbed the edge of a large, jagged boulder, burning hot to her touch. Breathing deeply, she rested there for a moment. Ahead of her, like a mirage, a young evergreen rose straight as a watchtower in the bright sunlight. Below it the crumpled red metal glinted.

She seemed alone in the world, suspended in time and space on the rocky cliff face over which the red car had somersaulted. The wreck was eerily silent; she heard only the grating of cicadas and the sighing of wind in the trees. A feeling of unreality washed over her. *How could I have got myself into this? It seems like a dream—a bad dream, someone else's dream, not mine.*

An image of Yves's laughing, handsome face formed in her mind, but she forced herself to concentrate. She had to hurry.

The sun hurt her eyes as its rays shattered on the broken metal and glass of the wreck. Grasping the supple young pines and willows, she made her way over the rocks, moving carefully but quickly now.

A final jump would land her on the narrow ledge where the car had crashed. This maneuver would be by far the most difficult to make. She would have to swing her body back and forth like a pendulum to get up enough momentum to reach, to the right and below, a rocky surface about two yards square.

She pulled with all her might on a clump of bushes, testing their resistance. The roots held solidly. She had a moment of fear. A miscalculation here would send her pitching into space over a dizzy drop of several yards, onto the jagged rocks below. She tried to take courage by reminding herself of her body's supple strength and agility, gained from years of gymnastic training. "*Now*," she whispered, and grasped the branches tightly. After a final hesitation her feet felt the emptiness.

As she swung her body in a wider and wider arc, the idea came to her that she was going to die: that this hallucinatory scramble down a sun-baked bluff, now rocking crazily about her, would be her last experience in this world. Fighting panic, she clenched her teeth and let go of the branches. She landed lightly and precisely on the ledge. She crouched low, her heart pounding.

She could clearly see the rear end of what was once a luxurious sports car. Strangely, it had landed right side up, perched on its belly, jammed between a tree trunk and the rock face in an almost normal position. The trunk had sprung open and she could see the case. Eagerly, she moved forward. But before she could grab the case, she drew back suddenly, involuntarily.

In sickening detail, she could see a man's arm dangling at a strange, dislocated angle from the driver's open door. She could see the red stain that had spread down the sleeve of the shirt and dripped in a small red river from the wrist. Startled, she shrank back.

Beneath her feet the rock face crumbled, throwing her off balance. She flung her arms out desperately, clawing for something to hold on to—something to stop her headlong slide over the ledge. Her hand caught at an edge of the rock, and her whole body twisted sharply. A wall of unyielding stone snapped suddenly into her field of vision, and in the same instant she was jolted painfully to a stop. With bone-cracking force, her head hit the rock. There was blackness and then pain.

She lay stunned and breathless. Through the roaring in her ears she could hear voices. They came from above, and very far off.

"Cut!" yelled Yves. "Cut, cut, *cut!*"

There was a confusion of orders and counter orders, curses and exclamations.

"Rosemary!"

"God, she almost went over!"

"Are you all right?"

Rosemary tried to wave. It was a terrible effort. She raised her arm, fighting the waves of pain that washed over her. Her head felt enormous. The sun was burning hot on her face and her whole body seemed to have been wrenched and bruised. Her arm was scraped from wrist to elbow where the fall had torn her checked shirt.

Long, slow-motion seconds passed as the mist cleared from her vision and the world came once again into focus. The sky was above her, calm and blue. Sheer sandstone surrounded her; she could smell the sweet, forest-cleansed air. She could hear people scrambling down the cliff above her. Stones skipped and rattled under booted feet. The branches cracked and rustled. Male voices filled with urgency called back and forth.

Some stunt woman I've turned out to be, she thought painfully, as she propped herself up on one elbow. The pain shot from temple to temple in her head, drumming mercilessly., The men scrambled and leaped recklessly, covering the last few feet to the ledge on which she lay. She could make out the voices of Louis, the cameraman, and Ben, one of the character actors.

"Hang on!"

"Don't move—we're coming," shouted Ben, huffing and wheezing with the effort of his descent.

Louis, younger and more agile, got to her first. "Just stay still, now. Have you broken anything?"

"No," gasped Rosemary, trying to smile. "I've banged my head pretty solidly, but I'm sure I can get up now."

"You gave us quite a turn," gasped Ben. "If you'd skidded much farther, you'd have gone over that twenty-foot drop. You took a big chance rushing down like that."

"I'm sorry. I wasn't timing it right, I guess." Trembling, she got to her feet. The pain in her head made her dizzy and she leaned heavily on Ben's arm.

I've really done it this time—wrecked another shot, and after all that work, she thought, angry with herself for being afraid of the "body" in the car. She had known all along it was a dummy soaked in hemoglobin, only real enough to fool the camera in a long shot. The long, tiring morning climbing up and down the bluff, angling her body so that Yves's camera could catch her movements to best advantage, planning each step—had all been wasted, because once the cameras were rolling, eating up all that expensive film, she had goofed. And her head felt as if she had cracked it open.

"Okay down there?" called Yves, leaning over the edge. Rosemary waved up at him.

"Poor Yves. He'll be sorry he ever hired me," she moaned.

"Don't you worry about him," comforted Ben. "Here, hang on tight now and we'll get you up this hill."

Together the three struggled up the rocky bluff like survivors of some battle. The men carefully supported Rosemary, who was beginning to recover from the shock of her fall. Her lithe young body responded well, and she was relieved that no serious damage seemed to have been done.

Hands reached out as they neared the end of their climb. They were pulled over the top and everyone cheered—everyone except Yves, whose handsome face was scowling and grim. Rosemary smiled wanly.

Ben, who was perspiring heavily, sat down abruptly to catch his breath. "Perhaps you should have carried *me* up the hill," he gasped.

"Are you okay?" Yves was beside her; his voice was tense. "You were moving too fast, Rosemary. And the script didn't call for you to lean into the wreck like that; especially not to jump back in horror. What on earth happened?"

"I'm really sorry...I don't understand it myself. It was as if I was looking at a real body. It was strange—spooky. There was no one around, just me and the wreckage. It seemed so real. I don't know. It was a shock, just for a moment, that's all."

Yves put his arm around her. His blue eyes were warm and laughing again. "What an imagination! You'd make a great actress."

"I'm really sorry if I ruined the shot," Rosemary said.

"It's all right. We'll piece it together in the cutting room. Do you think you can do the next scene?"

"Sure, I...."

"Okay, let's get on with the next scene!" Yves shouted, directing the technicians back to their

places. The machinist once again got ready to sus-
pend the mobile platform supporting the main
camera, with Yves and the operator, out over the
drop.

Stupified by her headache, Rosemary felt completely removed from these preparations. She was
still overwhelmed by fear, still identifying with her
fictional role so much that she could not bear the
thought of going down the cliff, of facing the terror, again.

"Camera!" ordered Yves.

Clapper in hand, an assistant entered the camera's field. Rosemary turned back toward the set
and noticed that Yves was climbing onto the platform next to the cameraman. She automatically
walked over to the edge of the cliff, where her
vision plunged downward to the rocks below.

At a signal from the director, the assistant
opened the hinged board upon which was written
the title of the film, as well as the numbers of the
scene and the take. With a dry clack he dropped it.
Registered in the sound track to mark the start of
the take, the clap had, as it did on all movie sets, a
magical effect. Conscious of his responsibilities,
each participant, from the most humble extra to
the star, immediately got into his role and became a
sort of robot whose gestures had been pro-
grammed by the director.

The sound of the clapper provoked a different
reaction in Rosemary's body. She shivered involuntarily and stood rooted to the spot, unable to move.

"Cut!" yelled Yves. Before the platform could be
lowered completely, he leaped to the ground and

ran over to Rosemary. He grabbed her arm and turned her around to face him. "Hey, come on now—you said you were all right!"

"She can't handle it," whined Lola, who had rushed forward. "I told you, Yves, you'd get nothing but trouble using amateurs."

"Shut up, Lola," Yves snapped.

Rosemary, bewildered, looked around her at the group of technicians and assistants. To her, their faces held only blame and recrimination. The film was progressing without a hitch, and even if it was only a B film, the whole crew believed in its financial success and counted on seeing it make the commercial circuit before the end of the year. And now, by some inexplicable stubbornness, this novice was going to slow down its completion.

"I'm really sorry to let you down," she faltered.

Louis spoke up. "You banged your head pretty badly," he said.

"Yes," said Ben loudly. "She should rest. We all should rest." There were murmurs of agreement.

With a sharp gesture, Yves silenced the group. Very tenderly Yves touched Rosemary's forehead. She winced with pain. "Yes, I see now. There's a swelling starting. You'd better lie down for a while. We'll shoot around you."

Gently he steered her through the watching group of actors and crew. Lola, the star of the film, sat a few feet away in her canvas chair. As they passed, Rosemary heard her say, rather loudly, "I thought we were pushed for time around here."

Yves ignored her and helped Rosemary to the trailer dressing room. "Lie down, darling. Just shut your eyes and don't think about anything." He helped her to stretch out on a couch and awkwardly dabbed at her scrapes with something from the first aid kit. Then, very softly, he brushed her cheek with his lips. "I'll check in on you later." She watched him, the sun gleaming on his golden head, as he smiled and quietly shut the door.

She lay very still on the daybed, nursing her bruised forehead with a cold cloth. She felt very foolish in spite of Yves's attempts to comfort her. Was he angry with her? She knew his money problems with the film were desperate; she wasn't contributing anything by messing up her small part in the work.

She felt a strong sense of being out of place—an amateur, and a clumsy one at that. Most of the cast and crew were tolerant enough. Some, like Louis, Alexander, the second director, Ben, and Marie, the wardrobe mistress, were even friendly and helpful. But many were aloof or hostile—they seemed annoyed that the director had insisted on hiring her. Rosemary now felt that they were right. What was she doing here?

"I want you close to me," Yves had said. She heard the words as if he had just spoken them, although it had been more than a month ago. Her head swam. Memories emerged, perfect, like patterns caught in a shifting kaleidoscope.

Yves. Stepping into her shop and into her life. Yves, tall, golden, tanned. With the blond beard and curls of a young Viking—and with eyes that were a penetrating, arctic blue. She had been buried for years, it seemed, in the wood-paneled book-

store that she had built on the shaky foundation of
her mother's small legacy. The hours were long,
the rewards marginal; perhaps she had looked a
little grim and businesslike.

Yves had stood directly in front of her, his open,
radiant smile filled with mockery. Even now,
remembering, she was flooded with a sense of
lightness. He seemed to have brought the sun into
the shop with him. Fontainebleau was a tourist
town and reasonably sophisticated, but it had not
prepared her for this shining, forceful young man.

"What can I do for you?" she had asked, summon-
ing her best professional manner and immediately
feeling foolish as the warmth of his gaze flickered
across her.

He waited a heartbeat or two, then spoke. "I'm
told, *mademoiselle*, that you have the finest collection
of books available in the Fontainebleau area." His
manner was courtly, a mocking response to her
careful decorum.

She had turned then, with a confused gesture,
toward the showy display of travel books designed
to interest the visitors who flooded Fontainebleau
every season as part of their Paris—Ile de France
itineraries. "We do have an excellent selection, sir."

"I'd better explain." His voice had dropped. "I'm
researching a movie—scouting locations in the
Forest of Fontainebleau. It should be something
fairly specific, about the forest itself."

Rosemary had pretended nonchalance. She
didn't want to seem impressed by the glamour of
the film world. "Well, then, I imagine some of these
road guides would help you quite a bit. Here's one

with a number of photos of scenic spots in and around the forest."

An impish grin played around his mouth. "We're also interested in the châteaus and fine houses around here. A lot of the action has that sort of background."

Again he was standing squarely in front of her, holding her with his eyes. In spite of herself, Rosemary had felt her cheeks flush. It was apparent that their conversation really had little to do with books!

Why did she have the idea that he was laughing at her? His penetrating gaze carried a compelling message, and something within her responded, quite contrary to the sensible dictates of her brain. But she would show him that he couldn't walk in and bowl her over! She would keep the conversation on course.

"What sort of film are you doing?" she asked. It sounded flat, inane, but he responded with enthusiasm.

"It's a suspense thriller, adapted from a book that's really hot on the paperback lists right now." He turned to another display rack. "Here it is. *Count Reynard: Memoirs of a Gentleman Thief.* I got hold of the rights cheaply, before the publishers knew how well it would do."

At least this was something she could talk about. "It's a big seller all right, especially around here. Nobody knows who the author really is—but he seems to know Fontainebleau very well. And he seems to know quite a bit about criminal methods. We've had a lot of burglaries, very much in the style of the ones in the book."

"What a gimmick!" laughed Yves. "No doubt some little old librarian turned it out, neatly disguised by the nom de plume of Count Reynard."

Rosemary had smiled at the thought. "You're probably right. But I would have thought you'd know who wrote it, having bought film rights to the book!"

"If I did know, I wouldn't tell you, but I don't. It was all managed through lawyers. The writer can remain a mystery as far as I'm concerned, as long as it helps sell books. It'll sell my movie, too, I hope!"

Rosemary found that she was smiling openly at him now, warmed by his boyish enthusiasm.

He seized the opportunity and clasped her hand between his. His touch was warm and firm. "Look, my name is Yves, Yves Delorme. I've never seen you before in my life, but I want to see you again. In fact, I want to see you now. Have lunch with me."

Rosemary was a little taken aback. "Oh, I couldn't—that is, I don't usually . . . ."

"You look as if you work too hard. Do something you don't usually do. Come with me, please." He had assumed a charming humility, one that Rosemary didn't believe for a second, but the idea was hard to resist.

She hesitated. "All right. But I've got to clear up a few things." She hurried toward the rear of the shop.

"Hey," he called after her, "what's *your* name?"

"Rosemary Bally." She smiled and turned quickly into the shop's back room.

Bertha, the middle-aged woman who worked for her as a sales clerk-bookkeeper, fluttered about ecstatically as Rosemary hurriedly ran a comb through her long, honey-colored hair. "Did I hear him say he was a film director?"

In the mirror, Rosemary's green eyes looked back at Bertha with a certain vibrance. "Shame on you, Bertha! You hear absolutely everything!" she whispered. But she was blushing, and it emphasized the attractive dusting of freckles on her nose and cheeks.

"Listen, I'm delighted that you're going out on a date. Don't you worry about a thing around here, now. Have a wonderful time!"

"Stop being silly!" Rosemary said as severely as she could. Smoothing her dress, she walked back into her shop, which was a subtly different place, now dominated by the presence of this man who was to play a major part in her life.

They had lunched at *Napoleon*, opposite the magnificent Renaissance palace that gives Fontainebleau its name. Light filtered through a glass roof as they sipped a lavishly expensive wine. Yves talked eagerly and brilliantly, touching on many subjects. Rosemary was smiling and slightly bemused, watching him. He had such energy and enthusiasm.

His conversation sparkled with stories about the film business. He told her about his own career, which was just being launched. "But I expect to make my name with this film. I was lucky when I got the rights, and you can bet I'll make the most of it!"

Suddenly he seemed to check himself "But enough about me! I'm here to find out everything I can about *you*, Rosemary. What motivates someone as pretty as you are to poke around among dusty bookshelves all day?"

Rosemary had laughed. "Well, it's hardly that, you know. Bookselling is a competitive, sophisticated business. Of course, I was foolish enough to imagine when I got into it that I'd have lots of time to read! But there's plenty of challenge, and it helps if you do like books."

"You seem very young. Do you own the business?"

"Yes. I've sunk the capital from my mother's will into it. It wasn't much: the money was originally intended to get me through university, but I wanted to do something right away, something concrete that would give me independence. I was nineteen when I began...."

"I admire that. You're strong and ambitious," marveled Yves. "We could do things together, you and me." His smile was deep, warm and direct.

Hastily Rosemary went on. "It's been six years of very hard work. I must admit that we've barely scraped by. But things have begun to improve, though just recently."

Yves had leaned forward and taken her hands in his. "Listen to me. We're alike, you and me. There's even more in the world for you than this business you've created...."

Rosemary withdrew her hands. "Speaking of business, I really must get back to the shop." She spoke the words primly, but her heart was racing inside her. This incredible man had threatened to turn her whole world upside down in the space of a few hours, and Rosemary was not at all sure yet that she was ready for something like that.

Yves' eyes were mock-serious. "You can't do that, not when I've just discovered you! Let's talk some more, please."

Rosemary laughed lightly. "You artists are all the same. You think the rest of the world has nothing to do at all, except talk about schemes and plans the way you do."

He tried to look hurt. "These, my dear lady, are not mere schemes. One day you'll see my name in lights, up there with the famous. You'll be able to say you knew me when. But, if the call of commerce is stronger to you, there's nothing I can do, is there?" Gallantly Yves stood and offered his arm.

Rosemary could not help noticing the glow he seemed to spread around him. As they walked back to the shop, all eyes turned to them, watching this tall, blond warrior whose golden aura drew admiration from every side.

Rosemary had resolved to keep her feet on the ground. She wouldn't let him think she'd been dazzled like some foolish schoolgirl. As they parted, she offered a noncommittal hand to be shaken.

Yves had grinned very broadly and bowed his blond, curly head. "I'll be seeing you," he said firmly.

"Perhaps," she had replied, permitting herself an arch little smile.

Her coolness seemed to draw him to her. Again and again he appeared in the bookshop, talking brilliantly, ranging over every subject. The days had flown by during his visits.

Beautiful women openly admired him—gazed at him in the street. He was tanned, laughing and sure of himself. He had a million ideas and told her about them eagerly. He wanted this, he wanted that. He had a little money from a rich old uncle who had died; he had certain investors willing to offer more. The film would recoup their money a hundredfold. "I live only to finish that film. My head is filled with scenes, shots, dialogue. I'll show them—my film is going to take off."

His candid blue eyes had filled her with a dangerous tenderness. He brought excitement and a heady sense of freedom to her life.

"Freedom is the wine of life," he would say. "Since we were both born under the same sign of the zodiac, we must have the same tastes."

Over the next week or so, he had called on her several times, always whisking her off to some new and exquisite restaurant. The film crew had been moved into the area. Yves explained that they were doing exterior shots, using the spectacular cliffs and rocky outcrops in the forest of Fontainebleau. "You must visit us on the set," he said again and again.

One day he had an announcement. "I've been doing some serious thinking and I've got an offer to make you: Lola, our star, is blond and about your size. But she is very inept in the action sequences that require her to look the part of a woman who could track down a villain. I wonder if you would consider standing in for her in a few sequences?"

"But that's impossible! I've so much to do here. Besides, I've never done anything like that in my life!"

"From the way you're put together, and the things you've mentioned about your athletic skills—especially gymnastics, I know you'd be great at it. Come on, what do you say?" He had held her at arm's length and looked deeply, coaxingly into her eyes. "You've lived a tight, narrow life, Rosemary. You've worked hard, you've cared for your mother. You've never done anything for yourself. I know you think the little business you run is for yourself, but isn't it really for others, for your friends, the Arnauds—Thomas and his rich mother? For their approval? Say to hell with them, just for a little while."

His voice had dropped to a husky whisper. His sun-bronzed arms reached for her, drew her close. Rosemary closed her eyes and let her head rest against the strong muscles of his chest. It was like a dream. She smelled his warmth; it seemed like the sun, like open fields and skies. Suddenly he was kissing her. His mouth covered hers, firm, demanding.

"Do it for me if you must do it for someone. Come and let me show you what life can really be for you, for us, Rosemary."

She was breathless with the kiss, with the force of Yves's burning stare. "I suppose I can get away for a few days." The words were flat and faltering. She felt limp and tremulous, but struggled not to show it.

"I mean for us to be together, Rosemary. Together for a long time."

Again he kissed her deeply. Rosemary let herself feel the power of his desire. Did she feel the same way? She only knew that his kisses left her a little shaken, as though she were surrounded by a force she couldn't control.

It had been decided then. She would take a couple of weeks off.

Bertha, ecstatic, had reassured her about the shop. "Don't you worry for a moment, dear. It's about time you had some sort of break from all this. I'll manage very well."

Rosemary had had her doubts, but they were soothed by Yves's evident delight.

But business of filmmaking had turned out to be far from glamorous. Today's grueling sequence had left her battered and confused.

This sort of thing isn't for me; I've acted like a star-struck child, she told herself, rubbing her temples. The headache would not go away. Yves *had* seemed angry. The mounting costs of the day-to-day work must be getting to him. He wasn't always the sunny, magnetic Yves she had first met.

She had a sudden longing for home; for Clermont, the estate outside Fontainebleau where she had been raised. For the quiet gardens, the stately house and the old stables where she and Thomas had spent so many summer afternoons. She had an image of Thomas, in his library, patiently going over his books for hours, his hair falling disobediently over one eye.

The thought of Thomas made her feel faintly ashamed. What on earth would he think of her, swinging from trees and scraping herself on rocks, spending weeks with this scruffy crew of film people, and with Yves? He would be vastly amused, no doubt. Somehow that thought hurt her.

Rosemary remembered again Thomas's words of weeks before, when she had told him of her decision to work on the film.

"You're chasing rainbows again, Rosemary. The movie world is the antithesis of all you've known until now. You're not going to feel comfortable in it. Before the shooting ends, you'll realize your mistake—or else I'm wrong about you altogether."

Her face had been a mask. "Thomas, for once you're going to let me make my own decisions," she had said sternly.

Thomas had smiled bitterly at her. "*Your* decisions, Rosemary? Don't you think this movie, this adventure, belongs to your friend Yves?"

"Yves?" Rosemary's voice had risen. "What do you know about him? Really, Thomas, it's none of your affair, none of your business at all! It's beyond me how you figure these things out, buried here in your books. Or do you make a practice of listening to the back-fence gossip of Fontainebleau?"

Thomas's face had suffused with anger, but he contained himself with a visible effort. "All right I'll say nothing more about it. You're apparently bent on risking all you've worked for...."

Rosemary was seized by new anger. She had felt her cheeks burning as she lashed out at him. "All I've worked for! Yes! And you were the one who said *that* was foolish—that I'd never make the bookstore go—that I'd wind up wasting my mother's pitiful legacy. I'm sorry, Thomas, if I'm not perfect, if I don't measure up to the standards of the Arnauds. But I've tried and in a small way I've succeeded." She pounded a small fist on the table in front of her.

Thomas glared at her, but contained himself.

Rosemary's words tumbled out recklessly. She could bruise him, break his vast reserve, his remote superiority. "Yves, for example, is the first man I've met who's made me feel *good*, made me feel like a human being. He had confidence in me, Thomas, unlike you."

Thomas had erupted, his voice thunderous in the small room. "Yes, and he's overwhelmingly glamorous, the charming film director—a child of the counterculture who'll do anything to get what he wants—"

"And what can he want from *me*, I'd like to know? Surely you don't think I'm more enticing than all those sexpot women who fall all over him!" Rosemary had laughed then with heavy sarcasm. "I know. He's after my money!"

Her forced laughter fell hollowly into the silence as Thomas looked at her steadily. He had turned then, his shoulders hunched, to stare out the window. The moments dragged slowly, ticked off by the gentle old clock, and Rosemary's anger drained as her hasty words echoed mercilessly.

She had spoken then, timidly. "Thomas, look, I—I'm sorry. I can't explain it very well, but Yves has been good for me, he's made me feel...alive. Can't you understand that?"

After a long moment, Thomas had turned to her. "Yes," he said very quietly. "Yes, I can." His gray eyes, troubled, had held hers for a moment, then flickered away.

He had drawn himself up, very tall in the slightly disreputable tweed jacket, but somehow he looked battered. With a pang, Rosemary knew that she had gone too far, said something unnecessary in her rebellious anger. Tentatively she reached out, her hand trembling.... Abruptly Thomas turned, and then he strode from the room without another word.

Rosemary was uncomfortable now, remembering that conversation. Was she wrong, after all? Was she going against everything in life she really cared about?

A little sigh escaped her. No real answer came. She seemed to be divided—a person with a double personality!

Thomas had made this clear to her, and now his words touched home. Well, he could think what he liked, Rosemary told herself resolutely, sitting up on the sofa. He was too superior, too judging. She had decided long ago that she would have her own life, would show the Arnauds that she was more than capable of standing on her own two feet.

Right now there was a job to be done. She would go through with it, in spite of her still-aching head. She had been lying here in the trailer long enough. She found some aspirin and swallowed two of them.

Rosemary washed her face and put on one of Yves's shirts to replace the one torn in her tumble down the rock face. She stepped out of the trailer into the bright noon sun.

The crew was still busy, the grips moving heavy equipment, the actors off to one side working out their positions. Yves was pointing at a rocky ledge, indicating where he wanted the cameras aimed.

Few of them noticed at first the dark sedan that appeared, swinging off the road and then stopping beside the other vehicles. Lola turned languidly in her chair, shading her eyes. Yves, who was waving his arm to indicate a panning shot, stopped in mid-arc. The cameramen looked up from their work. The actors stood in their places, puzzled and alert.

"Looks like a couple of cops," somebody muttered.

Louis and Dany, the script girl, exchanged an urgent stare. Rosemary knew they were fond of certain illegal drugs. She saw Dany quickly step back off the staging area and walk with seeming casualness toward the actor's trailer.

There was an air of tension on the set as two men in beige raincoats got out of the car and walked deliberately toward them.

Chapter 2

The men surveyed the movie set with an air of cool authority. The raincoats, which were precisely alike, looked as though they'd been issued by the studio wardrobe department. They were not really necessary on this hot June day.

As they neared the group, Yves drew himself up to his full height, which was considerably greater than theirs, and stepped forward. "Is there something I can help you with, gentlemen?"

"Afternoon, sir," replied the older of the two, flipping his billfold open to show his identification. "We're from the district police commissioner's office. We'd like to ask you people a few questions."

"Just routine," said the second man, without expression.

"We're sorry to interrupt," added the first detective, his eyes surveying the scene. His tone was matter-of-fact and far from apologetic.

Yves smiled broadly. "You're not interrupting. In

fact, we were just going to break for lunch. What's it about? Our permit to film here in the forest is completely in order, so I know we're not breaking any bylaws."

"Nothing like that," said the first detective. "We're investigating a series of thefts and break-ins in the district. From the estates and country homes. Art thefts mostly. When did your unit arrive, Mr. . . . ?"

"Delorme. Yves Delorme, International Phoenix Pictures. That's my company. Yes, we set up the location about two weeks ago. The fifteenth.

"Just about the time the fun began, I'd say," remarked the younger detective with a humorless smile.

"Oh, really?" Yves was the picture of courtesy. "I'm afraid we don't hear much news out here. We've got phones and radios in the trailers, but to tell you the truth, we've been too busy for contact with the local scene."

"Mind if we look around?" asked the detective, who was already strolling toward the camera equipment, scrutinizing everyone as he went. The second man followed, lifting scripts, light meters, cameras, at random.

"We're at your service," called Yves, raising his brows ironically.

Rosemary noticed that no one was exactly indifferent to the stares of the policemen. Many stared back defiantly. Others were elaborately busy with the equipment. Lola sat with a hand mirror, adjusting her makeup. Dany made herself very small behind one of the technicians.

At last the detectives turned back to Yves.

"How many members in the company?" one asked.

"Twenty-three."

"They're not all there," said the younger one promptly.

Yves surveyed the group, counting aloud. "Twenty-two. Who's missing?" he asked the group at large.

Rosemary tried to think. Rolly, Dany, Max, Louis—Ben. Ben was missing.

Someone spoke up. "Ben Reay, the character man."

"Oh, yes," said Yves. "We have one actor off the set today. Reay is in town. Had to have a prescription filled."

"Describe him," demanded the young detective.

"Older guy, about fifty, five-foot-nine, gray hair...."

"Couldn't be," muttered the older detective. "Okay. Have you got a list of names?"

"Of course. But I can vouch for all these people. You can't suspect that hard-working technicians and actors have time to go around robbing châteaus?"

"We've got to suspect everybody, especially strangers. Consider the time element. You people arrived at just about the same time as the latest rash of crimes began."

"But why outsiders?" parried Yves. "Surely local people would know more about when the houses are unoccupied and what's in them to steal."

"That might apply to ordinary break-ins and vandalism," said the older detective, elaborately lighting his pipe. "But these guys have a pretty sophisticated system going. They take only the best stuff, and they're obviously working with the best fences in France. They use the forest for cover, probably.

"And whoever it is must be in terrific shape. Fancy second-story work. There's even a theory that it's one guy, a cat burglar. Don't subscribe to that myself."

The detective took the list of names that someone had fetched for Yves and ran down it with a practiced eye. "Nothing familiar here. Tell you what. I'll keep this if I may. Run it through headquarters for aliases or records. All right?"

"Certainly."

"We'll be going now. Thanks for your time," said the detective.

Yves, smooth and unperturbed, grinned at them. "If we notice anything or anyone unusual, we'll let you know."

The two men strode toward their sedan without thanking him.

As Rosemary watched them drive off, a number of confused ideas seemed to knot themselves in her mind. Thefts from the country homes of Fontainebleau...priceless objects very selectively stolen...a cat burglar...it all sounded very much like an exciting movie—very much, in fact, like the one they were filming right now! She had an image of the glamorous lone thief Count Reynard, fictional hero of a bestseller, dashing star of their picture...a played by Yves.

"It's too much of a coincidence," she said aloud.

"What is?" asked Yves.

"The movie burglaries and the real burglaries."

"I think it's a terrific coincidence. Think of all the free publicity!" He gave her a solid hug. "Hey, you're better now! Great. Let's have lunch."

Dany sauntered past, breathing an audible sigh of relief. Max and Louis grinned like mischievous schoolboys.

"A bunch of art thefts!" yelped Louis. "Just like the movies!"

Everyone laughed as tension was dispelled. They say down to lunch with general hilarity and bantering. Yves sat next to Rosemary, but got involved in a technical discussion and moved down the table. Then Ben appeared.

"Hey, you missed the excitement!" everyone cried, falling over themselves to tell him about the detectives.

"Ah, well," said Ben, "maybe next time...."

"Come and sit here, Ben. I want to thank you for rescuing me today," called Rosemary.

He took the empty space beside her. "Oh, it was nothing," he smiled. "The very least a fellow could do."

He had a pleasant face, which emanated warmth and something that seemed to her to be sadness. She tried to imagine his past. But it was he who asked about hers.

"I understand you're a local girl, Rosemary."

"I was born near here, and my mother and I lived for many years at Clermont, a very grand place," she smiled. "Actually, we weren't rich ourselves, but mother was a dear friend of the owners, the Arnaud family. We lived in the gamekeeper's cottage, in what is called reduced circumstances." She laughed lightly.

"You'd think such kind people would put you up in the fancy house," commented Ben dryly.

"Oh, I'm certain they would have done, but my mother always said that it was better for us to have our own place. It made us feel more like ourselves and somehow less dependent. Anyway, we had some money, not a lot, but enough to pay the expenses of the small place. So in a sense we *were* independent. As I grew older, I knew I preferred it that way. In fact, I don't live there anymore."

"And your father? Where was he all this time? Had he died?"

"Oh, he was something of a scoundrel. He ran off and left my mother when I was still too young to even remember him. I wouldn't say it was much of a loss."

"Don't you even wonder where he is?"

"I sometimes wonder what he thinks of himself."

Ben shook his head. "It's impossible to understand some of the things people do. But, happily, you seem to have survived very well." He smiled. "And what about your mother? You speak of her in the past tense."

"Yes. My mother died just over two years ago. She had been ill for a long time. She had a sad life. I don't think she ever got over that man. She married him against her family's wishes and they never forgave her. People were like that in those days." Rosemary smiled at him. "Surely you don't want to hear all this?"

"Go on," said Ben.

"Well, then he squandered all her money on mad escapades in the stock market. When it was gone he deserted her, and by this time she had had little me. Her family was not sympathetic. They just said, 'We told you so,' and left her more or less to her own devices, or so I'm told. She had a little money from my grandmother, but not enough to tempt any more fortune hunters."

"Quite a story. Sounds like something from another century."

"Really, it does, doesn't it? Of course, nothing like that'll ever happen to *me*." Rosemary's chin set firmly.

"No," said Ben lightly, "I'm sure it won't."

Yves interrupted them. "Rosemary, I've got to talk to you for a minute." He drew her away from the group. "Look something damned awkward has come up, darling."

"What is it? Can I help?"

"Well, yes, you can. Look, I'd never ask in a million years, but—well, I've got to get my hands on a little money, right away. You've got the shop, and I thought perhaps I could borrow—" He stopped, looking pained. "No, it's no good. I can't ask you to do it."

"No, wait, Yves. How much is it?"

"Only a couple of thousand—for a few days, that's all. Just until I can arrange a few things."

Rosemary's heart went out to him. He looked so terribly uncomfortable. "I'll help, of course," she said quickly. "I'll write you a check now. But I'll have to go into Fontainebleau just to make certain the bank account can take it."

He gave a slight smile and his eyes softened with a velvet sweetness. "No wonder I love you, Rosemary." He leaned toward her. "Or did you know that?"

Rosemary regarded him steadily. His intensity swept over her, but she managed a careless smile. "Well, we'll have to talk about that!"

"You know we will, darling—" Yves hugged her warmly "—and thank you! I knew you wouldn't let me down."

Rosemary was suddenly embarrassed. "I'll go now." She handed him the check. "I want to look in on the shop. I should be back in three or four hours."

"That's a promise," whispered Yves commandingly. His hand pressed hers tightly.

Rosemary ran back to the trailer. She removed her stage makeup, eyeing with dismay the bruise that was darkening her forehead. Hastily, she attempted to cover it with a little pancake and powder from the jumble on the dressing table she shared with two other women.

Then she put on her tan silk suit and combed her hair. Instead of tying it back as she often did, she tried to fluff it a little to cover the offending bruise. Then she collected her purse and left her makeshift little home of the past few weeks.

She started to wave to Yves, but he was immersed in a script and didn't see her, so she decided to slip away quietly. Most of the crew were still huddled around the lunch table and paid little attention to her.

Backing out of the parking area, she saw Ben in

the rearview mirror striding purposefully toward Yves. His expression was stormy. Pulling around, she glanced their way again. They seemed to be arguing. Ben was speaking calmly enough, but Yves seemed suddenly to become enraged. He towered over the older man and spoke with furious intensity, emphasizing his words with slashing gestures.

Rosemary wondered what the trouble could be. But it certainly wasn't her affair. She put the little car in gear and started down the road.

Just over half an hour later, Rosemary drove into Fontainebleau, past the fine old houses that clustered around the palace, many of them converted into aristocratic hostelries and restaurants. She liked to imagine the town in its days of Renaissance glory, when Francis I strolled the galleries of the château; or in the early nineteenth century when Napoleon, surrounded by pomp, completed the splendors of his House of the Centuries. Here the *Mona Lisa* found her first home in France, and here Louis XIV, the Sun King, stayed, surrounded by nobles and scented courtesans.

This rich patina of history was balanced by a layer of very contemporary chic. Paris was less than forty miles away. Parisians as well as foreign travelers came to Fontainebleau for its beauty, its art, its clean, scented air. Barbizon, Moret and Melun, picturesque towns dotted around the region, were also magnets to visitors. They featured medieval spires and ramparts, stone gateways and houses overhanging the narrow little streets.

Rosemary's spirits rose; she enjoyed the bustle of town. Being on location for two weeks, seeing no one but film people, had been claustrophobic, she realized. She looked forward to getting into the shop again, even to tackling the problems, whatever they were, that must have come up during her absence.

Expertly she maneuvered the little car into a just vacated space in front of the shop. The Reading Room was tucked neatly between two other storefronts. Its window and display sign reflected Rosemary's feel for atmosphere: it was a real, old-fashioned bookstore, which invited customers to browse and talk—a refuge from plastic and neon. As always, Rosemary felt a little surge of pride: this was *hers*, created from her own dreams and ideas.

She was pleased by the efforts Bertha had made with the display window. But she noticed as well that the entranceway was perhaps a little *too* quaintly atmospheric: it was bordering on the decrepit and could use a bit of remodelling.

She frowned at the thought. This was no time to involve herself in heavy expenditures. The money she was lending to Yves would probably exhaust her available assets. She wondered if last month's receipts would cover the various payments she had to make. She must check over the books right away.

As she stepped into the shop, Bertha, fresh and neat, with her gray hair smoothed back into a chignon, was closing a transaction with a man who was carrying a voluminous package. She glanced at Rosemary, and her eyes shone with pleasure.

When the man had gone, she rushed over and gave Rosemary an impulsive hug.

"It's wonderful to see you, dear! How's the movie business?"

Rosemary's smile was a little forced. "Not as glamorous as you'd think!"

"Oh, my. Say, you've got quite a bruise on your forehead! What happened?" Bertha, as usual, began to fuss, taking Rosemary's bag, steering her toward a chair.

"I fell down a cliff, believe it or not." Rosemary told her briefly about the accident on the set that day. Bertha made sounds of dismay, but Rosemary brushed her concern aside. "Bertha, how are the books? I've got to run over them quickly, before I go to the bank."

"We're pretty well up-to-date. Has anything happened?"

"It's not a problem, I hope." She looked Bertha in the eye and took a deep breath. "I've promised to lend Yves some money."

"Oh?" Bertha frowned. "I should have thought he'd have plenty, with all his talk about big-time backers and complicated deals...."

"It's something about a lag in getting things signed and delivered...unforeseen production expenses," said Rosemary hurriedly. "Look, I'm going upstairs to the flat to have a real bath for a change. I'll take the ledger and check register with me."

"If you say so," replied Bertha doubtfully.

"Don't worry. It'll be fine." *I hope*, Rosemary added to herself as she lightly ran up the back stairs to her studio.

Sun flooded the little sitting room decorated with plants and colorful prints. It was a far cry from the spacious, high-ceilinged rooms at Clermont— or even from the rustic comfort of the "cottage" where she and her mother had been officially quartered on the estate. But the studio, modest as it was, belonged to her, Rosemary Bally, and here she did not need to feel like some sort of poor relation. It was a relief to be back. *I'll just have a really quick bath*, she told herself. *The books can wait a half hour*. It would be good to pick up some fresh clothes, too, before she returned to the film location.

As she was running the tub her anxiety returned. It wouldn't take very much to upset her precarious financial position; she had begun her business on very little money and had relied on her knowledge of books, plus the comfortable surroundings of the store, to draw her share of trade. It had been a risky, sometimes harrowing, two years.

You can't just create a business overnight! She remembered Thomas's words. But Rosemary had determination on her side. Nothing anyone said could have stopped her—especially not the objections Thomas voiced. "You haven't enough capital; you'll lose it! Your mother did her best to hold onto her own little legacy and pass it on to you, to provide for your education. Why do you want to risk it all now?" he had raged, stalking back and forth in the library at Clermont.

"I want to live *my* way, Thomas. I don't want to depend on the kindness of the Arnauds any longer. *I'm not like my mother!*"

Thomas had scowled even more darkly, his gray eyes stormy, a stray lock of brown hair falling over his handsome forehead. He had seemed, framed tall and square in the arched window of that book-lined room, like an immovable wall blocking the way to her future.

There was an unspoken accusation in the air: *No, you're not like your mother. You're like your father; reckless and fatally extravagant.*

But Thomas had not said those words. Instead he had softened. "Still the little rebel," he had sighed. "I can see you won't be deterred."

The little rebel. Rosemary smiled now as she climbed into the enveloping warmth of her bath. Thomas had called her that since her childhood. He was five years older than she, and Rosemary had always struggled mightily, impossibly, to match Thomas at all the things he had taught her to do—the things they had shared. Riding across the fields at Clermont, or in the Forest of Fontainebleau among the gold red leaves of fall, hurtling after the huntsmen and the hounds, shouting with joy.

Gymnastics: with Thomas she had learned to do the exercises they both loved; balancing on the parallel bars, tumbling and calisthenics. Sometimes her compact little body would perform better than his lanky, adolescent one, and she would crow with the pleasure of winning. Then he would bully and tease her until she'd fly angrily at him, flailing and slapping. "The little rebel," he would call her in mock fear. Then they would collapse in laughter.

Thomas had been like a big brother, accomplished and admired. Then he had gone away to school, returning only for vacations as the years passed. Rosemary and her mother heard glowing reports of his successes, and by the time he had graduated, Rosemary had grown up.

She had learned about the sadness and dependency of her mother's life on the Arnaud estate. The old times of friendship with Thomas were gone and could not return. Thomas had changed, too—his somber, intelligent gray eyes seemed to look at her from a great distance.

She had often found herself puzzled and embarrassed. What was going through his mind?

On her mother's death, Rosemary's determination had crystallized. If Thomas and his mother thought she would cling to them, they were mistaken. She would make her own way, taking nothing from anyone. And so her career as a business woman had been born, and with it a new life away from Clermont.

Mrs. Arnaud had approved. "Here at Clermont, the birds are free," she had told Rosemary. "Thomas should not try to hold you against your will nor tell you what to do. You'd just waste away." The words had been spoken lightly, but Rosemary thought they had reflected a deeper attitude, one of relief at shedding the burden of the abandoned Bally women.

Rosemary couldn't blame Mrs. Arnaud. Handsome, accomplished Thomas was "a good catch," she supposed, and no matchmaking mother would want an unattached young woman around, however familiar, to obscure the issue.

But in the two years since she'd left Clermont, Thomas had remained buried in his study, working on manuscripts and ignoring the eligible young ladies of the district. Whenever she visited he was courteous, but somehow remote. There was a stillness about him that seemed to overlie something deeper.

Sometimes she detected in his expression the flickering of something potentially explosive. But whatever it was, the energy remained always contained, and Thomas never spoke his mysterious thoughts aloud.

Rosemary had become drowsy in the warm tub as her mind drifted, but the slight, nudging pain of her bruised forehead roused her. The aspirins were wearing off. She gave herself a little shake—she'd better get at those books. She dried herself and put on a robe. After taking two more pain killers she got down to business.

A rapid examination of the accounts reassured her. The shop had been well managed in her absence. But the bank book told a different story. Though the business was solvent, there wasn't enough money left over to cover the check she had written to Yves. The specter of a bouncing check, of a destroyed credit rating, rose before her eyes and she felt sick with apprehension.

Rosemary wondered if she could possibly renege on her agreement to lend Yves the money. She decided not—to her a promise was a promise, and besides, Yves had assured her that he would need it for only a few days.

How could she get out of this predicament? No

one was going to offer her a helping hand; to ask anyone for a loan would be impossible. Thomas, for example, would berate her for being foolish and extravagant. The bank? Her line of credit was stretched to the limit. She had no collateral.

Then she remembered one last resource, a packet of small bonds, saved for absolute emergencies. That was the solution; she would use them as security for a short-term loan at the bank.

Quickly she dressed and went back down to the shop. She was feeling refreshed now, pleased at having got herself out of a scrape. Bertha was stacking a new arrangement of books in the window.

"Do we have any of Thomas Arnaud's books on display, Bertha?"

"Not really. Why?" Bertha looked puzzled.

"I sort of thought we might."

"Listen. In thirty-five years of bookselling, I've learned a few things. The Napoleonic Wars just aren't summer reading. I'm displaying the usual— novels, travel books, thrillers. That's what people on holiday are interested in. With all due respect for Thomas Arnaud—who's a fine scholar, indeed—sales of his books just don't warrant the space. Now if he wrote detective novels, something like this little bestseller *Count Reynard*, we could relax and give him all the space in the store."

Rosemary laughed. "I doubt if he's ever even *read* a detective novel. But at least he's a local author. Let's give him a little display anyway."

Bertha cocked a speculative eye at her. She smiled. "Sure. Why not? I'll give him a corner in the window, maybe even a dashing photo of the author. All right?"

"Right!" Rosemary waved happily as she hurried off to the bank. The manager was cooperative, and funds were quickly made available to her.

Now that everything was taken care of, she should get back to the location, she supposed, but she was reluctant to return immediately.

Before going back, she decided to take a walk. She strolled toward the palace of Fontainebleau and its formal gardens. June was ending in a profusion of flowers and verdant grass. After the past weeks spent in the wild, forbidding beauty of the forest, it felt good to be among the orderly green lawns and the multicolored rhododendron bushes.

As she walked, she recalled another garden. At this time of year the roses would be enveloping Clermont with their perfume. She pictured Thomas, pruning shears in one hand and a basket in the other, carefully cutting the blossoms of his favorite flowers.

One day she had teased him about his passion for roses and had told him that gardening was a good pastime for retirement.

In answer, Thomas had picked a splendid rose with a pearly heart, whose petals were tinged with purple. He had given it to her, explaining that nowhere else in the world would she find one like it. He had created it by crossing two other strains and was still working to improve it.

"Have you named your creation yet?" Rosemary had asked as she carried the flower to her nostrils.

"I'm calling it 'Miss Bally'."

"Because it isn't perfect?" she replied with a hint of irony.

"Perhaps," Thomas had answered with a smile.

It was rare to discover these small chinks in the armor of his reserve. He was the very opposite of Yves, who was so open and expansive. *They're like sun and shadow*, she thought to herself now.

But why was she comparing them? Yves, smiling and compelling, had walked into her life and laid his love before her. Thomas, on the other hand, had never been anything but cool and correct, had never shown the slightest emotional interest in her. He had merely tried, she thought angrily, to run her life!

She sighed aloud. It was time to go. She returned to her car and was just starting the engine when Bertha rushed from the shop and waved frantically at her. Rosemary opened the car window. "What is it?"

Bertha hurried over. "A phone call from Clermont," she announced. "You've got to call there immediately. Thomas says it's *very* important!"

Chapter 3

Thomas's voice over the telephone was firm. "Rosemary, I'd like you to come to Clermont. This evening."

"Why, Thomas? Is anything the matter?"

He hesitated. "Perhaps you're not aware that you've been ignoring us for some time?"

"I've been busy."

"With this movie-star business, I suppose."

"Thomas, I'm not trying to be a movie star. I'm acting as a stand-in, a double. I do stunts for the star."

"You ought to give it up. It's risky—you could break your neck." His tone was severe.

"You seem to forget just how agile I can be. I'm doing it more or less as a favor to someone, a friend."

"Some friend, asking you to risk life and limb," he replied sardonically. "Look, I don't want to argue. You must come to the house this evening. Do you want me to come and get you?"

"Why is it so important, Thomas?" Was she expected to drop everything just because he had called?

"You'll just have to take my word for it, Rosemary. It *is* very important. I want you here, tonight. Come for dinner, why don't you?"

"Well, I've got several things to do. I don't know if I can. . . ." Rosemary was wavering—the inviting image of Clermont, with its fragrant gardens and quiet, glowing rooms, was vivid in her mind. What a contrast to the gritty trailer world of the film set! But what would Yves say? He was expecting her.

"I know you can come," persisted Thomas. "Are you worried about this boyfriend of yours—Yves? Surely you don't let *him* tell you what to do!" Thomas's tone was teasing now. Next she would find herself raising her voice at him, the little rebel of old.

"Oh, all right," she said. "I'll come. But you won't need to pick me up. I'll drive."

"Okay. But watch that lead foot on the gas pedal. You don't want to be collecting traffic tickets."

How annoying he was! "I'm as good a driver as you are, Thomas. What time?"

"Anytime. Right away, if you like. I'm going out for a while, but mother is here, of course. Better make it before dark, all right?"

"Yes, yes. See you later." When she had hung up, a thought struck her. How did Thomas know so much about what she was doing, about Yves? Bertha, of course! That kindly fount of information! She smiled ironically. Now she would have to bear his lofty contempt for the gypsy people of the film world, answer questions, explain herself. Well, it was none of his business, any of it.

It was nearly closing time for the shop. Bertha bustled about, elaborately busy, trying to give the impression that she hadn't overheard.

Rosemary sighed. Bertha meant well. How could she know that Rosemary hated to risk Thomas's questions, his criticism? She could hear his scornful words, even now.

"First, the gamble of the business. One risk. Now you're jeopardizing even that with this new escapade."

Nevertheless, there was something comforting in the thought of Clermont. She realized suddenly that she was very tired. She would welcome the peaceful embrace of the old house. It was a place in which to be quiet, to gather strength. She wanted very much to go there.

What should she do about Yves? The rocky area of the forest where they were filming was many miles from Clermont, which stood on the opposite rim of the huge 40,000-acre wood. It was at least a half hour drive back to the set, and then another hour through the forest to Clermont. She would be very late getting to the Arnaud's if she returned to the set as she had promised. "I'll just phone him and tell him everything's fine. He won't worry then," she said aloud, picking up the phone again.

Yves answered his trailer phone in an abrupt voice. "Yes?"

"Yves—it's me, Rosemary."

Immediately his tone changed. "Darling, I thought you'd be back by now!"

"Yves, I won't be back tonight. I'm going to stay with friends."

"Where?" he asked, his voice suddenly sharp.

"At Clermont, at the Arnauds'."

"I see." He was silent for a moment. "Well," he continued, in a more normal tone, "I'm sure you'll enjoy yourself. Look, are you going to be driving through the forest?"

"Of course. There's no other way."

"Can you stick to main roads?"

"For part of the way, but...."

"I'm just worried about these reports of criminal types who are supposed to have been lurking in the woods. You'll be careful, won't you?" he asked tenderly.

"I'm certain there's nothing to worry about, Yves."

"Just the same, I want you back with me, safe and sound, tomorrow."

Rosemary laughed. "I'll try."

"I do love you, you know," he said huskily.

Rosemary felt a hot flush slowly climb up her cheeks. Embarrassed, she tried to change the subject. "Hey, I saw you having a fierce argument with Ben. What was wrong?"

"You saw us?" Yves faltered. "It wasn't terribly serious, but maybe I'll have to let him go. The old fool wanted something I didn't. Something in the film. Doesn't seem to realize who's the director around here."

"Oh," said Rosemary. "Well, I'd better go. The bank's okay for the money, by the way."

"Oh, great. And thanks very much."

"See you tomorrow."

"Right." The phone at the other end clicked off immediately.

Bertha was peering at her over the counter. "So. Two of them, I see," she teased.

"Two what? You're a terrible old gossip, Bertha," laughed Rosemary.

"Can't help it. Now you be careful on those roads. They meander all over the place. It's getting on; it'll be dark soon. It really is true, I hear, about strangers coming and going in the forest at night." There was an anxious note in her voice. "How's that head?"

"Fine, as long as I take an aspirin now and then. Now everybody stop worrying!" Rosemary threw up her hands in mock desperation.

She drove out of town and settled into a cruising speed on the main highway and soon relaxed as she leaned back against the seat. Night had begun to fall and she switched on her lights. The evening was soft and the breeze from an open window riffled her hair. She lost herself in pleasant thoughts of Clermont, of dinner, probably with an excellent glass of Bordeaux....

In her rearview mirror, she saw one of the headlights following her suddenly detach itself strangely from the line of cars. It moved closer—a motorcycle, of course, with red running lights.

The police.

The machine drew abreast of her, as she checked the car's speedometer. She was traveling just under the limit. What could he want? Glancing to her left, she saw there were two of them. She drew over to the shoulder and stopped.

The two motorcycles flanked the car. One of the riders stepped up, suddenly opened her door and shone his flashlight on her. Blinded, she quicky shaded her eyes with her hand. The light dropped away and he raised his index finger to his helmet. "Your papers, please, miss."

As Rosemary turned to reach for her purse, which she had put on the backseat, her tawny blond hair fell across her face. She had left it down, but the identity card showed her as she usually looked at the store, with her hair obediently pulled back and held in place by a wide band that covered the top of her forehead.

As the policeman's eyes moved from the photo to the original, he asked suspiciously, "Are you really Rosemary Bally, twenty-five years old, who owns a bookstore in Fontainebleau?"

"Yes, sir," she agreed, giving him her most charming smile.

He waved the little pocket folder that she had handed him. "This has only your driver's license and an identity card. Where are the car ownership papers and the insurance certificate?"

Rosemary's smile disappeared. She rooted around in her purse, wondering what she could have done with the precious documents. She could picture herself in the bookstore, putting her license carefully together with her cash and keys, ready to leave. Had she had the other papers then, too? Perhaps she'd put them down on the counter and forgotten them.

The second policeman had opened the passenger door and now leaned into the vehicle and opened

the glove compartment. "Here's what you're looking for," he said. "You don't seem to know where
you keep your papers. Does this car really belong to
you?"

"Of course it does. I'd forgotten where the papers were. I've been rushed all day...."

"Call it in, Mark," said the first policeman. The
radios on the motorcycles squawked and crackled.
The officer spoke into the microphone and received
a static-filled message in return.

"This is the license number, all right," he said to
the first policeman. "But the rest doesn't add up.
The ID's okay, and if she's who she says she is, the
number must be wrong."

They stepped away and conferred in lowered
tones. They made a few radio calls and waited for
replies.

Impatiently, Rosemary tapped her nails on the
wheel. What could be going on? The policemen
seemed in no hurry to enlighten her.

At last one of them came to her window again.
"I'm sorry, miss. Looks as if there's been a mistake.
We've got extra patrols on, trying to catch some
burglars, because we received a tip that a car with
your license plate number would be carrying a certain big-time fence to a rendezvous in the forest
tonight. Looks to us like the tip was a phony."

"Yes, it must have been," Rosemary replied frost-
ily. "I hope I can go now."

The policeman handed her the papers. "Yes,
ma'am, you can." He grinned broadly, increasing
her indignation, but before she could think of anything withering to say, he bowed slightly and was

gone. A moment later, the two motorcycles raced off, their red lights disappearing in the dark ahead of her.

With an effort she focused all her attention on the road. She'd been delayed over half an hour. With the night erasing all the landmarks from the forest road the way seemed endless.

She was unsettled by the encounter with the police. Their talk of criminals in the forest made her nervous and edgy. She found herself imagining that the dark trees hid sinister secrets, that they were waiting somehow to envelop her. The sense of menace was increased by the loneliness of the highway—few cars appeared in either direction.

She shivered inwardly. *I'm tired. I must get hold of myself.* All this talk of cops and robbers and anonymous tips was affecting her, making her behave like a schoolgirl. *The tip.* Who could have telephoned the police about the car? But that was wrong. It was all a mistake—the police had said so.

Still, she wanted to hurry, to get to Clermont as soon as possible, to be out of this dark night, safe in the calm of ordinary, orderly living.

Suddenly she decided to take a shortcut. To Rosemary, the myriad side roads of this part of the forest were familiar ground. She had explored them on horseback and bicycle many times. If she left the main road and took a less traveled route off among the trees, five hundred yards after that she would turn onto a small road that led to the avenue where the Arnauds lived. It would save a great deal of time.

Arriving at the crossing, she hesitated for a

moment. It was getting late. Unlike the highway, where cars passed all night, the little road dissecting the forest became deserted as soon as dusk fell. At that quiet hour deer and even wild boars wandered about as freely as cars did during the day.

However, after the unpleasant interlude with the police, Rosemary felt less confident to drive on the highway than through a forest that had always been her friend.

Making up her mind, she turned off under the trees. The beam from her headlights lit up the leaves of the bushes that lined the sides of the road. An owl, its feathers the color of pearl, flapped heavily across her line of vision before disappearing into the darkness. Rosemary braked to avoid a startled rabbit, which zigzagged in front of her wheels.

She lowered the window and with great pleasure inhaled the sweet perfume of flowering acacias. She felt a deep attachment to this particular corner of the world. Her roots were here, and whenever she returned she always felt the same feeling of completeness. Once again happiness filled her heart, leaving her so euphoric that she drove right past the turnoff to Clermont.

It wasn't until she arrived at a crossroads where one of the forest rangers' houses was situated that Rosemary noticed her error. She knew it wasn't serious, however. From this center point eight roads and two paths fanned out like spokes from a wheel. Some of them came out, eventually, at diverse points in the immediate environs of Fontainebleau. She could even follow one of them to Clermont without having to backtrack. It was a rugged, little-used track that ended at the rear of the estate.

She noticed that a new sign prohibited automobiles from entering the road she wanted to take and that some construction work to block the entrance had been started.

But because the cement hadn't yet been poured, Rosemary decided to take it anyway. She drove cautiously, for the way was sandy, narrow and bordered with large rocks that made it impossible for two vehicles to pass each other. The way was so tricky and little used that it was refered to in the Arnaud household as Devil's Detour.

The road darkened ahead of her and the trees seemed to close in tightly. She pressed the switch to turn her headlights to bright, but their range was then too long and high. She went back to the dimmer beams.

But what was that, reflected in the momentary flash of the high beams? There must be a car in front of her. Its lights were off, for she couldn't see any red taillights. The road twisted sharply at that moment and she concentrated on the wheel.

She slowed to a dead crawl; she hadn't remembered even Devil's Detour being this bad. Experimentally, she flicked on the high beams once more. There it was, a glint of metal up ahead—several hundred feet away, she judged. The car obviously was not moving.

Lovers, she thought, smiling. *They're even crazier than I am.* She switched back to low and crawled cautiously along the road. In a few moments the beams picked up the car ahead. *A little less than half a mile,* judged Rosemary, *and I'll reach Clermont.*

She flashed her lights, hoping the other car could move enough to let her pass. It was in vain; the other vehicle remained where it was. She squinted and leaned forward. She could make it out more clearly now: rear bumper, license plate, trunk lid. But the trunk was open and the car was tilted at a strange angle, as if it had gone off the road abruptly. She stiffened. There was some kind of trouble here.

Rosemary stopped her car, hesitated, then got out and walked into the beam of her headlights. Immediately the peace of the forest enveloped her. The heavy air was filled with mysterious sounds, but she recognized them all as the long-ago companions of her childhood nights. The creaking of branches, the rustling of leaves in the wind, even the far-off hooting of an owl had nothing in them to frighten her.

Taking courage, she approached the other car. The accident was more serious than she had at first believed. The hood of the car had been caught sideways under the nose of the rock, which had smashed the windshield. The driver's door was open.

Carefully, she walked toward the open trunk. There was something familiar about the black attaché case she saw there. It was almost exactly the same as the one in the scene they'd been filming that day!

Rosemary felt her heart begin to hammer. In the darkness, she was enveloped by a strange tingling sensation. Her senses were heightened: she was as aware as a forest animal of her surroundings. She seemed to hear her own pulsebeat.

The glare of the headlights on twisted metal and shattered glass mesmerized her. Mechanically, like someone in a dream, she walked forward, bent down and looked into the interior.

Abruptly she felt as if she had been hurled into the past. In spite of the darkness inside the car, she saw again the horrifying vision: a corpse, bloodied beyond recognition, sprawled grotesquely on the stained seat, with one arm dangling, dripping blood, from the door.

Her eyes dilated with terror and she choked back a scream. The nightmare image, imprinted in her brain on the rocky cliff ledge that morning, returned, slamming into her mind in a crazy montage—the car, the blood, the corpse. It couldn't be; this was not real! Her head began to throb.

She gripped the car with both hands: the cool metal was real. She wasn't dreaming, nor was she making a movie. The victim wasn't a dummy smeared with hemoglobin, but a real man.

A dead man.

Rosemary fought to quell the unreasoning, screaming fear that held her. The man might *not* be dead.

Awkwardly she leaned into the car, trying to ignore the pounding of her heart, the pain in her head. She could not see the man's features, only the outline of his head, bent at a sharp angle, and the shirt, covered with a dark black stain. Trembling, she touched the wrist. Was the flesh warm? Was it cold? She couldn't tell. She couldn't find a pulse. Suddenly panic seized her again. She pressed a fist to her mouth. She must get help quickly.

She turned toward her car. Suddenly a shadow moved among the trees. Her heart seemed to stop. *Someone had been watching her*. That someone ran now, swiftly, disappearing deep into the woods.

I won't give in to panic, she said to herself. *I must hold on, I must get help*. The chaotic jumble in her brain focused quickly on that one thought.

Galvanized out of her dreamlike state, Rosemary moved swiftly. She remembered the forest ranger's house at the crossroads. She would go there, get the ranger, and phone the police.

She got into the car and locked the doors. Backing down the road, she drove as quickly as she dared, while her yellow headlights picked out in high relief the deep ruts and jutting stones of Devil's Detour.

Chapter 4

Breathless with the exertion of steering all the way down the road in reverse, Rosemary finally reached the crossroads.

The ranger's cabin was completely shuttered and shrouded in darkness, except for a single crack of light that pierced one of the windows.

Rosemary stumbled from the car and ran up the steps. Pounding on the door, she was startled by the sudden furious barking of a vicious-sounding dog. It was locked inside, to her relief, and she waited for someone to open the door.

There was no sound except the snarling rage of the animal. She knocked again, more loudly.

Abruptly, the light inside the house went out.

Rosemary pounded repeatedly, trying to shout above the animal's hysterical barks. It was no use. Whoever was inside had chosen to remain there.

Discouraged, Rosemary sank in a heap on the steps, her head on her knees. She felt weak, enervated. Tears of frustration started to her eyes and she sobbed aloud.

But this would never do. She raised her head, brushing tangles of hair from her eyes, and took a very deep breath. She stood and walked back to the car, with the watchdog's terrible din still surrounding her.

Once inside the car, she could sort out her thoughts. If the forest ranger wasn't going to help, she would go on to Clermont. It was the next closest place. She started the engine with an angry roar and headed for the road she had missed earlier—the road to Clermont's main gates.

The dashboard clock read twenty minutes to ten.

Ten minutes later she approached Clermont along the familiar avenue and saw that the stone-mounted gates were open. Swiftly she steered the car around the broad drive to the garage and parked. Mrs. Arnaud's stately old sedan was in its usual place and Thomas's more recent but utilitarian model was beside it.

Rosemary threw open the door of her car and ran toward the main house. A few lights cast rainbow beams through the stained-glass windows and onto the balustraded terrace. The French windows of both the salon and the dining room had their blinds closed, but the entrance door was flung wide open and the hall was brilliantly lit.

With a little cry of relief, Rosemary ran up the steps and inside. Breathless and nearly out of control, she almost collided with Mrs. Arnaud. Rosemary stopped in her tracks, trembling uncontrollably, unable to speak.

"Rosemary! Good heavens, what is it?" said the startled woman. "Here, come, sit down." Rosemary let herself be steered into the salon. Her whole body seemed to be shaking violently. She was still unable to say a word.

Mrs. Arnaud's cool gray eyes examined her closely. "But you're exhausted. Sit still. I'll get Alice."

Dimly Rosemary saw her carefully groomed figure, dressed as always in black, hurry out of the room. She closed her eyes, pressed them with shaking fingers. Surreal images of blood, of torn steel and glass, rocketed through her mind. They seemed to dance, to slip into slow motion....

VOICES CAME FROM very far away.

"Good heavens! What should I do, get water?"

"No, no, Alice. Rub her wrists—let's get her feet up on the couch. That's it. Now the pillow, here, behind her head. That's better."

Rosemary struggled against the pain and opened her eyes. Faces were looking down at her.

Down? She must have fainted!

"I've never done that before," she said. The words sounded small and foolish. Her own voice was as far away as the others.

The faces were worried, familiar: Alice, who had been housekeeper at Clermont since Rosemary's childhood, and Thomas's mother, Mrs. Arnaud.

"See. She has a bad bruise—there on her forehead. And a bump," said Alice.

Mrs. Arnaud tipped Rosemary's chin gently toward the light. "I see. How do you feel?" she asked.

"I've got a headache," mumbled Rosemary, closing her eyes against the glare.

"How did you hit your head, child?" asked Alice.

"Perhaps she's had a concussion," said Mrs. Arnaud gravely. "I think I'll call Dr. Benet. Have you been dizzy at all?"

"Sometimes...but I must tell you—"

Mrs. Arnaud didn't let Rosemary finish. "Rest," she commanded. "I'll go and call the doctor."

"I'll be all right," Rosemary began, but the woman hurried from the room. "Alice, you must listen to me. I saw someone out on the road...."

"Hush, child; you're making it much worse," soothed Alice.

The room seemed to spin around her. Rosemary closed her eyes. Her head was still swimming. *The man on the road, who had gone over the cliff...I must get to the car, get the brief case...I mustn't fall on the rocks...Yves would be angry. The sun is so hot...I'm spinning, I'm going to fall...there's blood!*

Abruptly she opened her eyes. That wasn't it! There was *another* man, in the car on Devil's Detour. A dead man.

Rosemary looked at her surroundings. She was here, safe at Clermont.

No one was in the room. Calm pools of lamplight lay on the carpets and burnished the carved wood of the furniture. In this serene place it was hard to believe the horror of her night drive in the forest.

She would have to find someone. With great effort, pushing against the deep, soft cushions, she sat up and got her feet onto the floor. She felt light-headed, queasy. Her arms and legs were like lead.

Where was everyone? And what was the time? Rosemary tried to clear her mind. She forced her body to respond and stood up shakily. She walked toward the door of the salon. The dizziness abated a little, but her headache was as persistent as ever. She passed a smoky oval of mirror. In it she saw a white-faced figure, a person with hair the tawny blond color of her own, and shadowed, frightened green eyes. She stopped and stared.

"I look absolutely dreadful," she thought. But it didn't matter right now. She smoothed her hair back, wincing at the pain from the angry bruise that marred her forehead.

As she stepped into the hall she heard a voice from the room opposite. Mrs. Arnaud was talking, apparently on the telephone. Rosemary overhead only a few words.

"...good. You'd better get here just as quickly as you can. Yes. Goodbye." Before Rosemary had made up her mind to cross the hall, Mrs. Arnaud appeared. She seemed a little tense.

"There you are," said Mrs. Arnaud, startled. Her mouth seemed to twitch, but she forced a smile. "I've been on the telephone...to the doctor...." For the first time in Rosemary's memory, Mrs. Arnaud looked nervous, unsure of herself. "He'll be on his way directly, I'm sure. But what are you doing wandering around like this?"

"Mrs. Arnaud, it's important. I have to tell you what's happened. We've got to phone the police."

The older woman's hand flew suddenly to her throat. "The police! But why?"

"I saw an accident on my way here."

"An accident? Where? What sort of accident?"

"On Devil's Detour. A car had hit one of the rocks...."

"Rosemary, you'd better sit down again."

"No! It's terribly urgent. A man was killed!"

Mrs. Arnaud drew her insistently toward a chair. "You saw an accident on Devil's Detour?" Her brow creased deeply. "I can't understand that."

"Why on earth not?" asked Rosemary a little sharply.

"Oh, what I mean is—what were you doing on *that* road, of all the roads to Clermont?" Mrs. Arnaud was nervously twisting the beads at her throat.

"What does it matter what I was doing there?" Rosemary cried. "I took a shortcut, that's all. What matters is that we report it right away!"

The older woman made a placating gesture. "All right, all right. Try to calm down, my dear. We'll speak to the police right away, if you like." She frowned and took a few steps back toward the study, where a telephone was kept. She paused, however, and turned to face Rosemary. She seemed to have made some decision.

"Look, Rosemary. I'm worried about something. Are you *certain* you saw an accident? I mean, you did receive a hard blow to the head, one which had made you dizzy and uncoordinated...."

"Mrs. Arnaud, I know what I saw. I may have got a little bruise, but it hasn't made me have hallucinations."

Of course the accident had been real, of course she had seen the blood-covered man...hadn't she?

She remembered how, in those shocked moments in the dark, the accident on the forest road and the one in the film had become confused in her mind.

"Thomas will be home very shortly. Will you do me one favor and wait until he gets here before we do anything? He'll be here any minute, I promise."

Mrs. Arnaud's tone was persuasive and Rosemary felt some of her anxiety drain away. Thomas! Yes, he would take care of it, would help her, tell her what to do. "All right," she sighed, suddenly feeling very weak and vulnerable. She glanced at the clock that stood farther down the hall. It was well past eleven!

Thomas's mother looked relieved. "Let's get you freshened up. You do look as though you'd seen a ghost!" She smiled coaxingly. "Why don't you let Alice give you a bit to eat and a glass of port?"

Rosemary remembered that she hadn't eaten a thing since lunch. She wasn't hungry, but knew she should eat something to build up her energy. She certainly had none now! She felt drained and limp, lost in a welter of confusion.

"Let me wash my face," she said with a wan smile. "Then I'll eat a little bit, if you insist. Do you have any aspirin?"

"Come, then, come with me," said the older woman, smiling for the first time since Rosemary had arrived.

Alone a few moments later in the echoing marble of one of Clermont's huge bathrooms, Rosemary held a steaming cloth to her face and tried to relax. She wondered why Thomas was out at this hour. He had been so insistent that she hurry to Clermont, that she be there for dinner, in fact. But he wasn't even home! Irritation welled up in her. It was just like him to issue a command, to insist that she come running at his slightest wish, and then not to show up himself. What on earth could he have wanted to see her about?

Feeling a little better, Rosemary went to the dining room and let Alice fuss over her with fruit, cold cuts and fresh-baked bread. She couldn't eat much, but found comfort in the polished wood and crystal that gleamed around her here in this normal world. The port warmed her and the nightmare images were soothed from her mind.

Rosemary welcomed the quiet and solitude when Alice had bustled back to her kitchen. Mrs. Arnaud did not appear, and Rosemary was just beginning to wonder where the woman might be when she heard the front door open and close. Footsteps sounded on the tiles of the hall floor.

She turned in her chair to look through to the hall. Suddenly Thomas was standing in the dining-room doorway. His face was partly shadowed. It seemed like one she hardly knew—strong, almost brutal angles cut down from his brow and cheek-bones. She stared at him for a moment, sensing from him a powerful wave of tension. His whole body—the broad shoulders under the summer shirt, the stance he took gripping the door frame— seemed to contain something urgent.

He returned her look, but she could not read his eyes. For some reason, Rosemary felt a little tremor go through her body.

Nervously she spoke. "Thomas, I've been waiting for you!"

"You have." It was a statement. He strode into the room, his dark brows knitted in consternation. "I'm sorry. I meant to be here earlier. I was held up."

He turned toward her, into the light of the chandelier. The brutal shadows she'd just seen on his face were softened. The lines at the corners of his mouth were perhaps a little deeper, and something about the eyes had changed, but basically his finely chiseled, intelligent face was the one she knew so well.

Suddenly she remembered. "Thomas, something's happened—an accident on Devil's Detour."

He looked startled, but said nothing.

"You've got to help. We've got to phone the police. I saw a body, a man's. We've got to do something about it. I've wasted more than an hour already...." The words were tumbling out almost faster than she could form them.

"What were you doing on that road?" he asked, his voice sharp. He began to stride back and forth.

"Why, that's just the same irrelevant thing your mother said!" Rosemary cried. Just then Mrs. Arnaud entered the room.

"Thomas, how glad we are you're back. Rosemary's had some sort of horrible experience."

"So she's been telling me." Thomas rubbed his jaw thoughtfully as Mrs. Arnaud repeated the accident story again.

"But," she added, "Rosemary's had an accident herself. Just look at this bruise!" She gently brushed Rosemary's hair from her forehead.

Thomas scrutinized the bruise carefully.

"I was wondering if she'd well, imagined things.

I've called Dr. Benet," Mrs. Arnaud went on doubtfully. "He hasn't come, and it's over an hour."

"Probably some emergency came up," said Thomas.

"I don't need him to come," said Rosemary very firmly. "I think we should do something about the man in the car."

Thomas looked at his mother for a long moment. Finally he spoke. "I think it's most unlikely that there'd be any sort of accident on that road, Rosemary. It's under construction. No one uses it. Are you certain you really saw an accident?"

"I saw the car, the blood, a body. I touched it as I stood there. I don't see why you don't believe me!"

"We're just worried that you might have had a concussion," said Mrs. Arnaud hastily.

"Please don't go on about the bump on my head. If you won't take me seriously it doesn't matter. I'm going to phone the police anyway!" Angrily, Rosemary rose from the table.

"And another thing—there was someone else there, in the woods. I don't know who it was; a witness, someone hurt in the accident, or who. But I have the feeling it was someone the police should know about. We've delayed so long they'll never find the person! It's my fault for being so weakkneed earlier, but I'm going to do something right now!" She started to leave the dining room.

Thomas stepped in front of her. "Wait," he commanded. Rosemary glared defiantly at him.

"All right," he said at length. "We'll do something right now. I'll take you to Devil's Detour and you can show me this wreck you say you saw. If it's true, we'll get the police right away."

It was something concrete, at least. "Fine, let's go," Rosemary replied.

Thomas brought his car around, and they drove through the dark labyrinth of forest roads toward Devil's Detour. Riding along in the rather spartan vehicle, Rosemary remembered that he had not had his car with him earlier this evening. Where had he been without it, she wondered. One couldn't go anywhere in the country without an automobile. She was tempted to voice her curiosity, but Thomas, silent at the wheel, seemed absorbed in thought.

They reached the crossroads and drove right through the construction, as Rosemary had done. The gouges and ruts bounced them around as the tires bit into the sandy road surface.

Rosemary peered anxiously into the darkness. They would come across the accident soon. She steeled herself, unwilling to face again the horror and the blood. She felt increasingly tense and fearful.

The drive lengthened. Surely they should have come upon the wreck by now—but the rocks all looked the same. Rosemary could not tell exactly where they were, but as the minutes passed and no car appeared in the headlights, her throat began to tighten.

This new fear was even greater than her apprehension at the thought of seeing the disabled car again with its horrifying passenger.

Now she realized something even more profoundly frightening. *The car was not there!* Each passing moment of the winding road drummed it into her head. Soon the back wall of Clermont appeared. There had been no accident on this road. Shocked, she turned to Thomas. He gazed at her steadily, but said nothing.

In silence, she turned her eyes back to the road. She stared, unbelieving, unable to accept what had to be the truth.

She had imagined the whole thing!

Chapter 5

Thomas and Mrs. Arnaud spent much of the next hour talking with Rosemary. They seemed deeply concerned at her fear and distress over the strange nightmare experience in the forest. Perhaps, they said, she had been influenced by her role in the movie.

"It's an exciting adventure for you, isn't it?" asked Mrs. Arnaud, handing her a glass of cordial.

"Don't exaggerate. I was only a double."

"But it must be strenuous—and you did fall down that rock face," said the older woman.

"My head is fine. It doesn't even ache anymore and the swelling's gone down. You're mistaken about a concussion. You'd better tell that doctor not to bother coming." Rosemary walked restlessly back and forth.

The elegant room, so quietly separate from the shadows outside, made the terrible immediacy of her experience fade a little. Here she could get a focus on reality.

Rosemary put her empty glass on a little table and looked around her. It was difficult not to feel soothed by the peace that this welcoming room emanated. All the furnishings—carpet, art objects and furniture—evoked the eighteenth century.

Thomas had completely transformed it, keeping only the lovely, authentic pieces among the antique furniture of his parents' day. He had very sure taste and a passion for old things. Rosemary saw that the woodwork had been repainted in an antique gray, and that new pale blue damask curtains framed the French windows.

"Rosemary," said Mrs. Arnaud, breaking in on her thoughts, "you've always had a vivid imagination, you know. I remember when you were six years old you used to make up fairy tales to tell your mother. At twelve, to horrify Alice, you would relate, better than Edgar Allan Poe, gruesome tales about brigands and pirates."

Rosemary's fear that she *had* imagined the entire scene was not allayed by these reminiscences.

But the dreamlike quality of the experience, its almost precise duplication of the terrifying climb down the rocky slope—and even the fact that the car had disappeared—these facts, in the orderly atmosphere of the salon, did not entirely convince her that her experience was an illusion.

She truly felt all right now—alert and calm. She had to sort the thing through. There must be some explanation other than temporary madness on her part!

"I'm not *that* imaginative," she asserted, facing them.

Thomas and his mother—both tall, slender, dark, with identical gray eyes, though his were shadowed by a craggy brow, while hers were framed by a smooth, ivory forehead and impeccably arranged waves—stood watching her carefully.

"You *have* got all the qualities of a dreamer, Rosemary. You're impulsive and you like to dramatize things." Thomas's expression was ironic as he spoke. He had the same lofty superiority as always! Little Rosemary, the kid who didn't know what she was doing, ever—the extravagant dreamer and mad spendthrift.

She would show him, show his remote, aristocratic mother. She grew more certain as the moments passed that what she's seen had indeed been real. She must prove it to herself, prove it to them.

But how?

What really could have happened? Why did these two seem set against her?

"Thomas, why were you so long getting home this evening?" she asked, turning casually to examine a small object on the table. "When you called, you insisted I come for dinner. But you didn't show up until well after eleven o'clock."

Thomas answered without hesitation.

"I told you I'd be out for a while, Rosemary. I was delayed longer than I'd expected, that's all...car trouble." The last was added almost impulsively.

"I see." She did not turn to look at him. *Car trouble!* Didn't he realize she'd parked in the garage earlier, right beside his unused vehicle?

He was lying for some reason. Perhaps they both

were. Wariness stole over her. She would be careful of what she said to them.

Thomas began to pace. She turned and looked steadily at him.

"I see no reason to get involved further with this, nor to call the police," he said with a paternal air of having settled the matter. "The car and the 'body' disappeared, as if by magic. I think we can assume that you're the victim of some strange nightmare, the result of a number of factors. Let's go over it again. You saw, or think you saw, a car disabled on Devil's Detour, where nobody ever goes."

"Right."

"What kind of car?"

Rosemary thought. "Red. A Mercedes."

"Hmm. A short time later, all traces of same have disappeared."

A short time? It had been an hour or more. Time for a tow truck to come and haul the car. But no tow truck could ever negotiate the rocky, narrow road. She was certain of that. And it could not get through the concrete and wood frame construction that was underway at the entrance to the road.

Maybe someone had pushed the car off the road into the woods. This, too, would have been difficult. The rocks lining the road were steep in most places. Few gaps wide enough for a car existed.

Or perhaps the man wasn't dead at all! He had recovered, and somehow driven his damaged vehicle away himself. But that was totally impossible. There was so much blood....

"All right, the car disappeared," was all Rosemary said.

"And you say you saw a person lurking in the trees. Might that 'person' not have been some shadow, a trick of the wind in the trees? Was it a man or a woman?" Her interrogator stood looking down at her now, stern faced.

"I don't know," Rosemary replied. It *had* been a person, someone very swift and agile, someone whose shoulders were broad—a man! She shuddered even now at the thought of that silent watcher in the shadows. "I really don't know." She lied, looking him directly in the eye.

"To my way of thinking, there isn't any mystery," announced Thomas.

"Perhaps you're right," said Rosemary, attempting to sound resigned. "Fatigue and emotional strain are probably clouding my judgment." She smiled at him with an effort. "I'll go to bed now and try to forget all about it."

The worry evident on the faces of the Arnauds disappeared miraculously. Thomas was pleased and terribly attentive as they all went upstairs.

He's trying to make me feel like a fool and an invalid, Rosemary thought. "I'll let him think he's succeeded." She smiled very sweetly at him.

Mrs. Arnaud planted a quick kiss on her son's cheek and put unusual warmth into the hug she gave to Rosemary. "I've made up the Louis XVI bedroom for you," she said. "When you were twelve years old it was your favorite, remember? You should discover your childhood dreams there once again. Good night, my dear."

An hour later, stretched out between fresh sheets that smelled faintly of lavender, Rosemary tossed and turned. Her taut nerves refused to relax and her mind kept going over and over the events of the evening, particularly her last confrontation with Thomas.

Why had he insisted the forest accident was a product of her imagination? Why had he lied? Where had he been all evening? No answers came to her.

Tired of stewing over her problems, she finally threw back the covers and got out of bed. Feeling her way toward the window she pushed back the drapes that Mrs. Arnaud had closed. The trees and sky were melded together in blackness, for it was a moonless night. The wind had risen and the vegetation shivered under its rough caress. Rosemary went out on the balcony and leaned against the railing. The cold of the metal made her shiver, but she lingered, listening to the rustle of the leaves, the crack of branches and the trills of a pair of nightingales that returned each year to the same linden tree to rest. From the forest came the faraway hooting of an owl. She had grown up here, near the Forest of Fontainebleau, and as a child she had loved exploring it and getting to know its secrets and seasons. The woods were almost a symbol to her of freedom and of happiness. Even now, the ancient trees seemed to give her strength.

The old trees would have much to tell if they could speak, Rosemary thought. These very oaks, here for centuries, had seen the princes, kings and nobles of old France, who rode to the hunt after stag and boar—a savage rite that had survived the dark ages of Europe.

Whirling through the forest paths on fleet horses, accompanied by the cries of the dog pack and the full-throated brass of the huntsman's horn, the nobility wore doublets blazoned with the crests of great families—red, gold, royal blue flashed like jewels in the deep, murmuring shade. You could almost feel their presence here, hear faint echoes among the crystal birdcalls. As a child, Rosemary had dreamed of such scenes, of a dark prince in wine velvet, who leaned down from his horse.

The hunt was carried on still, in the twentieth century, with a certain amount of pomp and excitement. She had always loved to ride with Thomas on autumn weekends through the crisscrossing paths, over the hilly, unpredictable terrain, ducking low branches as they chased the hounds. Occasionally a wild boar was tracked down, but the hunt was shorn by law of the bloody finish of medieval days. The joy of it was simply in the exhilaration of galloping, totally free amid the noisy excitement of the dogs—in breathing deep the sparkling air, touched by frost—in the glittering challenge in Thomas's eyes as he urged her to go faster still.

Rosemary smiled at the memory. She had been blessed, really, to have grown up here, nestled so close to the great beauty and mystery of the forest.

And the forest was truly her friend. But tonight her friend had betrayed her. She sighed, staring out into the night, staring at the dark woods. Luminous stalks of birches scattered themselves among the scarred and brooding trunks of the old oaks, beeches and evergreens. The great woodland, some fifty miles wide, was crossed by the river valley of the Seine and by hundreds of roads. Some were superhighways and some secondary roads, others mere pathways. There were many rugged areas of open rock, sandstone worn by time into bluffs and ravines. This was why Yves had been able to shoot scenes in the forest. The rocks, many of which were gigantic, were used by mountaineering clubs to train members for even greater challenges. They were an ideal setting for the hair-raising scene in which Rosemary climbed down to the "wrecked" car.

They were almost *too* authentic a location, Rosemary thought, remembering her dizzy tumble down the rock face. She'd truly been very lucky not to have taken a much greater fall. Even so, it had been quite a jolt, she thought ruefully.

She wondered if she *could* have suffered a concussion, one that had affected her judgment.... Her forehead was still bruised, but she no longer suffered the dizziness and headaches she'd felt this morning. And her strange fainting spell had almost been forgotten.

No, a concussion would have been more obvious than that. Of this she was convinced. Whatever she'd seen, however distorted and magnified by terror, had still been *real*.

And no one was going to convince her otherwise.

Rosemary shivered again. She recalled Thomas's opposition when she had wanted to phone the police. Might there be a relationship between this behavior and the drama in the forest? Did Thomas know more than he was saying about what had happened?

At that moment, Rosemary's gaze drew in from the forest to the lawn below her. Patterns of yellow light, cast through windowpanes, fell on the grass.

Lights? At this hour? They were coming from the salon. Perhaps someone had simply forgotten to turn them off. Impulsively, Rosemary decided to find out.

She wrapped her deep blue velour robe around her, softly opened the door to her bedroom and flipped the switch in the upstairs hallway. The glow from the overhead fixtures made it light enough for her to see her way down the stairs.

Her bare feet made no sound on the thick carpet that covered the stairs. Halfway down she stopped. There *was* light coming out of the half-open door to the salon. She continued on down the staircase.

In the hallway she again stopped, alert and hardly daring to breathe. The house wasn't sleeping as she had thought. Two people, Mrs. Arnaud and Thomas, were talking in the salon. She could hear their voices, but was unable to make out the words. Softly, stealthily, she moved closer to the door. She stood still, straining to hear.

Mrs. Arnaud's voice sounded strained, almost as if she was in the grip of a violent emotion. "...And what did you do when you got home?" she was asking.

Thomas answered sharply, "What could I do? I left it in the trunk of my car."

"In the trunk! But that's so dangerous...."

Rosemary didn't dare listen further. She feared one of them would emerge at any moment. She turned around and quickly went up the stairs. She would rather have died than let them know she'd been eavesdropping! She felt herself flush with shame at overhearing the confidential dialogue.

But what was the dangerous object Thomas had left in the trunk of his car? More confusion! She crawled back into bed. Perhaps she could find out in the morning.

Little by little, the great peace that pervaded the house calmed her nerves, and she fell into a deep, healing sleep.

A concert of birds woke her the following morning. A few trees grew so close to the house that from her bed Rosemary could see only a little corner of the opal-colored sky between their branches. She knew it must still be very early, for the pink tint of dawn had so far touched only the tops of two majestic sequoia trees.

She got up and went out on the balcony. The fresh morning breeze smelled deliciously of damp earth and vanilla perfume, for a honeysuckle bush was climbing the wall under her window. She breathed in with pleasure and stretched like a young animal. Refreshed by sleep, she was able to smile at some of the terrors she had felt the evening before.

But then recalling the surprising words she had overheard when she'd gone downstairs, she wondered what it was that Thomas had hidden in the trunk of his car. The thought of finding out planted itself solidly in her mind.

Quickly she showered, put on a pair of jeans and a blue cotton pullover, stepped into a pair of espadrilles and tucked her long hair under a band. After a

quick glance in the mirror, she turned and headed
down the hall, unmindful of the fresh and lovely
picture she made even in this simple garb. Her
fitted pants emphasized her slender body with its
long legs and narrow hips. Her hairdo set off the
gracefulness of her neck. Her freckles, which to her
great dismay had been accentuated by the sun of
the past few weeks, added a youthful touch to her
face, with its wide green eyes.

The household was still sleeping. Making hardly
any more noise than a cat might, Rosemary slipped
along the corridor, down the stairs and into the
office, where she knew she would find, hanging on
a keyboard, the duplicate sets of keys to both Mrs.
Arnaud's and Thomas's cars.

In the garage she went around to the trunk of
Thomas's car, unlocked it and opened it. Thomas
had backed into the garage, which was so dark that
Rosemary at first couldn't distinguish anything
other than the spare tire set in its special cavity.
Mechanically she pulled at the tire, but it didn't
move.

She felt around and as her eyes became accustomed to the dark, she was able to pick out a light-
colored garment carelessly rolled up in the bottom
of the trunk. Rosemary picked it up unfolded it and
went to examine it in the light of day.

It was Thomas's Windbreaker, but what a state it
was in! It was covered with large brown red spots,
which had stiffened the cloth—spots too characteristic for Rosemary not to identify them with immediate shock. *Blood!*

She leaned against the car in shock. Her heart

hammered in her chest and a cold nausea swept over her. Horror widened her pupils as it had yesterday morning on the cliff face, and as it had the previous evening on Devil's Detour.

Blood on Thomas's jacket, a lot of blood . . . like the blood in the car, on the man's shirt, on his arm, dripping slowly. . . .

Blood connected Thomas to the accident! He had hidden this jacket, hidden it from her—and maybe from the police!

But why? Could Thomas be involved with something illegal? Calm, balanced, always in control, Thomas hated violence, and Rosemary would have sworn he was incapable of voluntarily hurting anyone.

On the other hand, he had lied last night. He hadn't had car trouble, because he hadn't been *out* in his car! Perhaps someone else had been driving him, someone whose car had ended up crumpled against a rock on a lonely forest road!

Fleetingly her mind formed a picture of the shadow figure, watching her in the forest. That person knew a good deal about the accident and that person had run away. It was frightening, inconceivable.

Had the shadow man been Thomas?

She remembered the strange glances he and his mother had exchanged, as well as the words she had overheard later. There was no doubt about it. Thomas had a secret, a terrible secret that he didn't want her to find out about.

Then bitterness and anger evaporated the horror that the discovery of the blood-spotted garment had caused. Whatever they were hiding from

her would not remain a secret for long! She would
find out for herself what was going on!

She rolled the Windbreaker up again and
replaced it in the trunk, which she relocked before
leaving the garage. Back in the office, she hung the
keys up in their proper place. The house was still
silent. Rosemary decided that she still had a good
hour of peace and quiet before everyone woke up.
She would take a walk through the woods to the
scene of the accident. By the light of day without its
shadows, Devil's Detour might tell an entirely different story than it had last night.

Chapter 6

Rosemary left the enclosed grounds at Clermont by a little door at the back of the garden and found herself very near the entrance to Devil's Detour.

The branches of oak and pine trees met to form an archway of greenery above the road. The way was so narrow that in certain places Rosemary had the impression that she was going through a tunnel.

Farther on, sunlight flecked the rocks and the full-grown trees were replaced by bushes. The pale green leaves of the birch trees scattered a multitude of patches against the vault of the sky, while scarves of morning mist still wrapped themselves around the silver trunks.

Rosemary was deeply affected by the beauty that surrounded her. Walking in the forest always made her feel a deep, joyful peace. The lacy pattern of a fern, or dewdrops catching a ray of sunlight, seemed to her more exciting than the most marvelous works of human artistry.

She walked briskly for a quarter of an hour until she estimated she was in the general area of the accident.

At first she had a difficult time finding the exact spot where she had seen the red Mercedes the evening before. She wondered once again if she hadn't really dreamed the whole scene.

Horseback riders, up even before Rosemary, had passed by. The hoofprints of their horses obscured the tire tracks in the sand. The rocks along the road all seemed to look exactly alike. She could find no visible traces of the car. Even with its smashed windshield and crumpled hood, it had indeed disappeared into thin air!

Anxiety washed over her, submerging her like a wave. Was she a prisoner in a world that was only a parody of reality—like a reflection caught in a mirror? But then, like a wave that rolls back after crashing on the sand, the anxiety left her. Her eyes registered two details: at the base of a rocky bank some clear tire tracks were visible, and lying beside them, slivers of broken glass caught the sun. She had found what she was looking for!

Even if she still couldn't explain the car's disappearance, she was now certain that it had existed— outside her own nightmares.

She stooped to pick up the glass and suddenly thought better of it. If Thomas knew more than he was saying about the accident, if he was trying to convince her it hadn't happened in order to cover up some secret of his own, then it wouldn't do to let him know in any way that she'd been sleuthing. He might come back to this spot. She left the glass where it lay.

But there must be some way to find out how the red Mercedes had disappeared. Rosemary pondered her next move.

The forest ranger. She would go to his cabin and this time force him to respond to her knock. *I'll wait all day if I have to—he must know something,* she thought to herself.

She set out for the crossroads, walking briskly down the rutted track, surrounded by the gentle sounds of the forest. The pure forest air seemed to lighten her step.

Maybe the ranger will be more cooperative during the day, she thought optimistically. *I suppose he had his reasons for turning out the light last night. Perhaps he's as scared as the rest of the people around here, with the heavy toll of vandalism that plagues the country houses.* It was inviting territory for thieves: summer homes, many of them converted mills and renovated farms, were common targets for pillaging.

They were relatively isolated and contained the belongings of well-to-do Parisians who were seldom in residence. And there were many old estates, similar in scale to Clermont, with its valuable antiques and select furnishings. Churches were robbed, too, indicating that the vandals would stop at nothing. Fear was a common and realistic response to the situation—the thieves hadn't hesitated, on several occasions, to use physical violence on unlucky homeowners who surprised them at their work. Many people had taken to locking themselves in at night.

Plunder. Rosemary thought about the rich trove that awaited accomplished burglars in the Fontainebleau area. They seemed to know their business well, these bandits. They made night forays into unoccupied homes where the many gadgets such as expensive cameras, appliances, radios and televisions—so beloved of petty thieves who could easily get rid of them in city pawnshops—were ignored in favor of rare and usually priceless items, not so easily sold.

Tapestries from Brussels, woven in the jewel tones of medieval guilds; exquisite porcelains made by the craftsmen of Sèvres or Limoges; glittering enamels by Fabergé; gold and silver from Florence; paintings by masters from the Renaissance to the Impressionists. And jewelry: diamonds, rubies, sapphires—the heirlooms of families who had passed them down for generations, or baubles proudly acquired by the recently rich. Even the furniture in many of these homes was virtually beyond price, designed by the great craftsmen of the seventeenth and eighteenth centuries, and lovingly preserved with beeswax and lemon oil. Treasures of the very rich, or of those who were no longer rich, but merely clung to beautiful things that carried the fine patina of age and tradition.

It seemed a cruel violation that the stately homes, these rooms so quiet in their classic elegance, should be invaded and mercilessly looted. People were increasingly wary, it was true, purchasing formidable locks and guard dogs, but the thieves seemed unstoppable. They carried on their daring trade right under the noses of the police. Each time there was a lull in their activities and the affluent settled into a false security, they would strike again.

Rosemary heard almost daily talk of it in town. Each time a new robbery occurred, thought of Clermont jumped to her mind. Fear that the burglars could not fail to be attracted to the old estate would grip her. She imagined the dark figures stealthily prowling the ground, silently scaling the stone walls, breaking into the serenity of the timeless rooms.

The furniture, much of it from the Directoire period, would be brutally seized and carried off. The delicate porcelains that were Thomas's special pride would be evaluated by cold and calculating eyes. Alien feet would trample the aged but still glowing carpets, and gloved hands would quickly, silently slice the oils from their frames.

These images were unbearable to Rosemary. Clermont was the home of the Arnauds, representing for centuries a symbol of order and civilized values. It was somehow her home, too; a background from her childhood and a comforting haven from a world that moved swiftly and heedlessly into an age of disposable machines, disposable values, disposable people.

Perhaps Thomas was right, she thought, to immerse himself there, steeped in the lore of an earlier time. The Napoleonic period: it was filled with grandeur, with the glories of war, of ceremony. Yet that time seemed remote, of interest only to those as scholarly, as remote as Thomas himself.

Sometimes Rosemary found herself wishing that Thomas would live a little more in the here and now. Why, for example, was he so belittling of everything she did? Yes, she was a woman of today, capable of striking out and succeeding on her own. It was necessary that she do so. Yet Thomas had said that she was wrong to risk everything on her business. How wrong *he* had been—as she was proving!

Clermont was his, with its security and its traditions. Rosemary had known for years that she must make her own true home, somehow, away from the alluring security of Clermont. She could not bear to feel dependent. Clermont was the symbol, in part, of her mother's dependency and unhappiness. It carried an aura of home, but also an air of the established, superior world to which Rosemary really did not belong.

She blushed suddenly. Had she had a fleeting, shameful thought—that the burglars who might attack that world and shake it were secretly to be admired? No, she would not admit such a thing to herself, though more than once it had been bandied about on the film set. After all, what they were doing was essentially a caper movie, which glorified the adventures of a gentleman thief. The classic have-nots of the film world—and all those who'd go to see the picture, as well—found the idea marvelous. Everyone liked to see the applecart jiggled a bit, if not upset.

Rosemary sighed inwardly. She had to admit that she shared some of those feelings. The count's glamour, his dark, exciting make-believe world were vivid in her imagination. His best-selling memoirs proved that nearly everyone enjoyed a secret admiration for the sort of man who broke the rules and lived by his own.

It meant danger. And romance. And a heady excitement. But it was stuff for the movies, Rosemary reminded herself.

She wondered again about the striking similarities between the movie—the fiction of Count Reynard, the gentleman thief, and the events in the real world.

It was a small literary puzzle, the fact that the novel had been written under a false name. Yet it nudged at the edge of Rosemary's mind. What if the writer used a false name for the simple reason that he was, in fact, a thief?

It's not so absurd, Rosemary told herself. This writer knew a very great deal about robbers and their methods. And about the exquisite art treasures in which they specialized.

What a game it would be to a certain daredevil sort of man to commit these robberies and then write about them! The thefts had been going on for years, although this current rash had, it was true, been too recent for anyone to have published a book about them.

The police were deeply concerned. They were combing the area, treating even the film people as suspects. But when would they have time? Yves seemed to be driving everyone twenty-four hours a day!

However, she reminded herself, she had hardly kept track of everyone. They bedded down in the camper-trailers at night, the women sharing some, the men others. She could only account for the comings and goings of Dany, the script assistant, and Marie, the wardrobe mistress, with whom she shared accommodations. The others might well have carried on all sorts of activities!

There was, however, only one *fact*. The police had said that the newest round of thefts had begun about the time the film company had arrived. And that was a coincidence, she was certain.

Rosemary decided to hurry. Her confusion was only deepened by these musings. She would put them out of her mind. As for Clermont, well, it was safe. No burglars had yet tried to break its peaceful shell.

Suddenly she stopped in her tracks. *Why not?* Why had the estate remained untouched? It was reasonably isolated, and its many treasures were among the finest of the region. It was strange that no one had tried to invade it. Thomas even made a habit of leaving the main gates open—and at all hours.

It appeared that he felt immune to the possibility of thefts. It was just one more example of his superior attitude, Rosemary decided.

Or was it something else?

Rosemary forced the thought from her mind, not wanting to face the growing suspicion of what that something else might be.

She turned her mind to the task ahead of her. Would the ranger be able to tell her anything? Even locked inside his house he must have heard something. Once again she reflected that he could hardly be blamed for being afraid. . . .

Nevertheless, the man was a forest ranger. It was his job to help out if emergencies occurred in the forest, whether at night or not. He shouldn't have been cowering in his cabin and refusing to answer her desperate summons. Rosemary set her jaw. He would not get around her this time! The crossroads was in sight, and with it the little wooden house of the ranger. A few chickens were scratching around the yard in front of the house. An old woman, wrinkled and with a kerchief tied around her head, was tossing them grain from her gathered-up apron. She responded to Rosemary's greeting and willingly exchanged a few banalities about the weather.

If the woman lived permanently in the house, she could not possibly have been unaware of the drama that had happened within earshot last night. Rosemary tried to prolong the conversation. She made a few flattering remarks about the management of the farmyard and admired the peonies that were blooming between two beds of vegetables. "Peonies are my favorite flowers," she said. "Are yours very fragrant? I've never seen such lovely ones."

It was an innocent lie, for the peonies growing on the grounds at Clermont were tall and bushy, and the colors of their gigantic blooms ranged from light pink to dark purple.

Flattered, the old woman offered to pick her a bouquet. As she started cutting the blossoms, she gloomily talked on about the pains that were stiffening her joints. Rosemary listened to her distractedly, looking for an entrance that would enable her to steer the conversation toward the subject she was interested in. Then she remembered the barking dog that had made its presence known so vociferously the night before. Where was it today?

"Aren't you afraid at night in this secluded house?" she asked.

"Oh, yes," said the old woman. "Fortunately we have Duke, our German shepherd. He's a good guard dog and we let him sleep inside. My son— he's the forest ranger for this area—took him along on his rounds this morning. With the riffraff prowling around everywhere these days...." With a sweep of her arm she indicated the crossroads in front of the house.

"Except for a few poachers, who would possibly come here after nightfall?" Rosemary asked.

The old woman straightened up painfully and looked at Rosemary as she shook her head. "Crooks sometimes prefer deserted roads," she confided. "Last night, for example, not far from here, something funny must have happened." Absorbed by her memories, she broke off speaking but continued to wag her head from side to side.

Rosemary mastered her impatience with great difficulty and took her by the arm. "What happened?" she asked. "You're scaring me."

"Oh, don't worry. There's nothing to fear during the day. The police who tour the area on horseback do their job well and they come by frequently enough to keep hoodlums at a distance. But at night it's something else again. To be honest with you," she added after a slight hesitation, "I shouldn't generalize, because it's usually pretty quiet around here. But last night I was so afraid that I intend to go to the police about it. I'm just waiting for my son to come back."

Rosemary interrupted her. "Were you attacked?"

"Oh, no—thanks to Duke. When he started barking, the intruders, who must have guessed how big he is, didn't persist."

She stopped, seeming to be torn between the desire to talk and the need to keep her story for the police. Finally, she continued in a confidential tone.

"My son spent the evening at a cousin's house in Barbizon. I was sitting alone in front of the TV, and I had closed the shutters. It was about nine-thirty when the dog started to growl. I turned off the television, opened the living room window and listened. I'm getting a little hard of hearing, but I thought I heard the sound of a car engine. At that hour it was a little surprising."

"And then, all at once and very clearly in the silence of the woods, I heard a shot, a cry, and then a second shot."

A shot! Rosemary was riveted by the word. She barely heard the rest of the old woman's story. Gunshots meant that whatever had gone on on Devil's Detour last night was far more serious than even she had thought!

"I was glued to the spot, I can tell you," the woman continued. "Even if my life had depended on it I wouldn't have been able to move an inch, I was that scared. I waited for what felt like an age, with the sound of my poor old heart beating in my head. Duke kept growling and baring his teeth, so I plucked up my courage, opened the shutter a crack and peeked out. And I saw a car go by."

"Had the car been in an accident?" Rosemary asked, hoping her voice sounded normal.

"No, I don't think so.... It was backing up out of

that road that the Forest Department is in the process of blocking off. It turned around right under my windows, too. It was a sportly little car— very low and fast."

Rosemary was only half listening. *Shots*—they meant murder. The dead man she'd seen had been murdered, not killed in an accident. And Thomas was somehow wrapped up in this nightmare—this *murder*. No wonder he'd been so anxious to gloss over the accident on the road, to convince her that she'd seen a mirage. It wasn't an accident at all!

"Someone tried to break down my front door," the old woman was saying. "I was frozen to the spot, but Duke almost wore out his lungs scaring the killers off."

"Oh, that wasn't killers, it was me," Rosemary said—and immediately wanted to bite off her tongue.

The old woman was staring at her. She would go to the police, she would tell them her story, and tell them that she, Rosemary, had been in the area of the shooting. Then the police would come asking questions....

Rosemary went on impulsively, "I knocked on your door. I was trying to take a short cut and I got lost."

"So it was you!" exclaimed the woman, half-incredulous.

"And you switched off the light," Rosemary said in an accusing tone.

"That's right. But what do you expect these days? With all the robberies and crimes...." The woman lapsed into deep thought. With her eyebrows drawn together she asked, "But then who cried out? Not you, surely. And there were those shots. I certainly didn't dream them up."

Rosemary had to get away before the woman began to ask any more questions. It had been a blessing in disguise that she had not succeeded in rousing the woman last night. So far, she had not connected Rosemary with the crime to which she'd been a distant witness. No one but the Arnauds knew Rosemary had seen the dead man. There was nothing to connect Thomas to him, either. She decided to try to confuse the issue.

"A lot of things sound like guns going off. There are firecrackers, tires exploding or badly regulated exhaust pipes. And there's nothing to prove that a poacher hadn't let himself be tempted by a rabbit or a squirrel," she said.

The woman remained thoughtful. "Maybe I didn't really hear shots. Last night, when my son came home, he didn't want to believe me. 'Mama,' he told me, 'Ever since we moved to this secluded house you see bandits everywhere. It's become an obsession with you!' He had a great time teasing me because I'd made up my mind to go see the police commissioner. Now, maybe I won't. I'll think about it some more."

Inwardly, Rosemary was flooded with relief. The old woman had too many doubts about the shooting itself to wonder why Rosemary had *really* been in the forest. Perhaps she'd forget about going to the police—especially since there was no crumpled car on the road, no body for anyone to discover.

The woman wouldn't let Rosemary take the

heavy spray of peonies as they were, for they were drenched with dew. "I'll wrap them up in some paper for you, dear, or else you'll get your shirt all wet." She was still muttering distractedly to herself several minutes later as Rosemary, having thanked her for the flowers, walked hurriedly away.

The new facts she had discovered tumbled about in her mind. Shots, a murder. Could Thomas possibly be involved with such a thing? She had known him all her life. It was hardly credible.

The old woman had not seen anything that gave a clue to how the Mercedes had disappeared. But she'd admitted to being hard of hearing. Something more could have occurred near her house without her knowledge. She'd seen a sporty car take off quickly. That was easy—she'd seen Rosemary's car.

Rosemary asked herself what point there would be in carrying her detective work any further. She would only find out more horrors, more things she didn't want to know—that Thomas did not want her to know.

She was able to reconstruct the night's happenings, using the old woman's testimony. Someone, on that dark road, had plowed a Mercedes into the rocks after being shot. Why that man had been there, why he had died—these facts were not important. All that mattered was that she *had* seen a body. She was not going crazy, after all.

Then she stopped walking suddenly as a thought struck her. She had lied to the woman—lied instinctively and well—to try to keep her from going to the police. She had not been protecting herself, for up until that moment, going to the police had been more or less her own intention.

No, she had been trying to protect *Thomas*. The unplanned sureness of her action inwardly startled her. What on earth did she think she was doing?

A new realization followed. Rosemary was calmly certain that she must continue to try to get to the bottom of whatever was going on. She must know what dark meaning last night's events had for Thomas. She must know for his sake and—she was beginning to suspect—for her own.

A few moments later she slipped once again through the secluded door into the garden at Clermont. As she walked through the rose garden another problem came to mind. How was she going to explain her absence that morning? She had spent more time in the forest than she'd planned to, and by now everyone would surely be up and wondering where she was, for they knew she hated lazing around in bed. If she confessed where she'd gone, Thomas would undoubtedly guess the motive behind her walk. She wanted to keep her discovery to herself, for the moment at any rate.

She stopped to think. Taking a walk at dawn in the rose garden and around the rest of the grounds would be a natural thing for her to do. No one would question that explanation of her absence. But she had this cumbersome bouquet of peonies with her. What explanation could she give? The old woman had been so pleased to give them to her that Rosemary felt unable to simply throw them away.

She decided instead to get rid of the paper that was wrapped around them. Peonies grew in great abundance around the grounds of Clermont. She would simply say that she had felt like picking some.

Behind a hedge where she wouldn't be seen, she extracted the flowers from their wrapping. The old woman had used a local newspaper from the preceding week, and a headline drew Rosemary's attention: *Gang of Château Thieves Continues to Scour Area.*

With a strange, tingling sensation, Rosemary skimmed the article, then reread its conclusion.

...Some observers believe that the gang leader lives in the district, for the thieves are extremely well informed. Because they choose unoccupied homes, they can work in almost complete security. Furthermore, a characteristic of the gang is the very fine taste that guides their choice of loot. Only objects of great value are stolen. The agility of the robbers is remarkable, as well. To carry out their latest larceny, they had to let themselves into the house by an attic window, four stories up.

One troubling fact is that the fingerprints that the police found on the attic windowsill are identical to some found in connection with a recent theft of gold bullion. During that heist, an Air France jet transporting gold from Paris to Berne was robbed of its cargo. So far, no one has been arrested in connection with that robbery.

When Rosemary raised her eyes, the sheet of newspaper was shaking in her hands. She bunched it up and stuffed it among the branches of a bush, then picked up the peonies and headed slowly toward the house. She felt a strange new anxiety.

Her mind was starting to assimilate all the bizarre facts that were churning around in it. The pieces were falling into place. Suddenly she stopped stock-still.

The Paris-Berne bullion heist: she remembered following news coverage of the story. At the time of the theft Thomas had been in Switzerland!

Thomas's books about the Napoleonic era appealed to a specialized market, and as a bookstore owner she knew that the sale of his books alone wouldn't bring in enough royalties to support him, let alone run an estate like Clermont.

For the first time it occurred to her to wonder how the Arnauds actually did support themselves. Clermont required a lot of upkeep, as did its extensive grounds. The hired staff was composed of Alice, a full-time cleaning woman and a gardener. When Mr. Arnaud had died, word had got around that as a lawyer he had taken better care of his clients' finances than of his own. There was even a rumor that he might have been close to bankruptcy—conjecture that had been reinforced by the sale not only of his law practice, but also that of two buildings belonging to Mrs. Arnaud. Yet Mrs. Arnaud certinly led a comfortable, middle-class life. Where did she and Thomas get their money?

Rosemary had to admit that thievery wasn't the obvious answer to Thomas's invisible means of support. She told herself to stop letting her imagination run away with her. But the idea that Thomas was involved with art burglaries might explain his presence at the scene of a shooting, and it might explain why he lied so glibly about his whereabouts. She could easily imagine Thomas, with his impeccable taste, choosing the rarest objects from some antique treasure trove....

She was sickened suddenly by a heavy apprehension. What would she discover about this man whom she'd thought she knew very well? It was terrifyingly apparent that she did not know Thomas at all.

Ahead of her the house stood, its friendly old stones suddeny cold, gray, forbidding. Gathering her flowers to her, Rosemary walked slowly up the steps.

Chapter 7

As Rosemary crossed the entrance hall with her flowers, Thomas bounded up the steps and into the doorway. He had been immediately behind her! Rosemary wondered uneasily if he had been watching her.

Sunshine flooded in with Thomas, painting a rectangle of light on the black and white tiled floor. A big cedar, the branches of which spread generously over the terrace, formed a bluish screen against which Thomas's silhouette was outlined. Rosemary was struck by the force that emanated from him, by his air of authority. She couldn't make out his features, but from the proud, almost arrogant way he carried his head she supposed that he was savoring a sort of triumph.

He wore an old, worn riding outfit in which he looked perfectly at ease. The light emphasized the energetic bone structure of his face. In an automatic gesture, he threw back the lock of brown hair that always fell over his forehead.

"Ah—there you are, Rosemary!" His tone was filled with his usual courtesy and reserve. But as he moved closer, Rosemary thought she saw a vibrant light, a cold, radiant flame in his gray eyes. Looking at him, she was filled with a sense of strangeness, edged very slightly with something else. Was it fear?

"Did you sleep well?" he asked. There seemed to be irony in the question, as if he knew very well that she had crept around eavesdropping at a late hour.

She said quickly that she'd slept very well indeed.

"Let's eat, shall we? I'm starved!"

In the dining room the table was set for breakfast. The windows were open and from the grounds the singing of birds entered in a profusion of golden light. The air from outside flowed in, fresh and fragrant.

Taking her place opposite Thomas at the mahogany table, she discovered that a new object had been added to the room. A lovely Sèvres porcelain ewer rested on a console between the two windows.

She wondered where the vase had come from. Its value was very great. Has Thomas bought it recently? Or had he stolen it from a nearby château?

Rosemary caught herself. The assumption that Thomas might be a thief had certainly run away with her imagination!

She smiled to herself. The very idea of Thomas clambering about on château walls was absurd. The calm atmosphere of Clermont easily dispelled such fantasies.

"Why are you smiling?" asked Thomas, scrutinizing her face.

"Because of the ewer," she answered. She remained outwardly calm.

He raised his eyebrows in an unspoken question, so she had to explain. "I was telling myself that if it could talk, it would probably have some interesting stories to tell."

Thomas pushed his chair back, stood up and headed toward the console. He picked up the vase carefully, caressing the handle and the golden spout with his hand. He carried it to the window so that Rosemary could admire its deep blue color. Then he replaced it on the console.

"Where did you get it?" asked Rosemary.

"This ewer is a very rare collector's item—the only one like it in the world. It was created by the Sèvres porcelain works and was given to Napoleon at his wedding to Marie-Louise," explained Thomas, unfolding his napkin. "However, what makes it precious to me is the fact that it's a sort of trophy," he added with a malicious smile.

Rosemary felt her heart start to beat more quickly. "A trophy? That's strange!" she exclaimed.

"The addition of the ewer to this room is recent and was made in a way that was rather...unusual. Many people would be scandalized to hear how I got it. Its presence in my house symbolizes a conquest...."

He broke off. His mother had entered, followed by Alice, who carried a tray holding a silver coffeepot.

Dressed in a silk print robe and, as always, impeccably cool and elegant, Mrs. Arnaud had carefully brushed and put up her hair. It seemed to Rosemary, however, that fatigue and worry had printed deeper lines on her face.

"The day promises to be magnificent," said Mrs. Arnaud, once she was seated. "Rosemary has already taken advantage of it. At dawn I saw her run across the grounds like a colt frisky with its freedom. Did you have a nice walk in the forest, dear?"

Rosemary was gripped by a wary fear. It seemed impossible that the older woman should know about her excursion. Except for those of her own bedroom, the shutters at the back windows had all been closed when she had left the house. The grounds had appeared deserted to her, as well, and the door by which she had left was hidden behind bushes tall enough to screen it from view.

She responded in as casual a voice as she could muster, "I didn't get any farther than the rose garden. On my way back I stopped behind the outbuildings to pick a bunch of flowers."

"Ah, yes, peonies," said Mrs. Arnaud in a distracted voice. Then to Alice she added, "They're lying on one of the tables in the hall. Would you mind putting them in the two jade vases in the library?"

After the housekeeper had left she turned toward Rosemary again. "Will you do me a great favor, dear? I forgot my pills in the cupboard in my bathroom and I'd like to take one before breakfast."

"I'll go up and get them," Rosemary said, getting to her feet. She left the dining room and turned to go upstairs. Abruptly she stopped. Alice had gone off to the kitchen with the peonies. If she stayed right where she was, she'd have a chance to hear what these two would say to one another this morning.

She was eavesdropping again! Everything in Rosemary's upbringing told her not to do it, but a stronger need won out. With one eye on the door opposite, in case Alice returned, Rosemary did her best to hear what Thomas and his mother were saying.

"Stop worrying," Mrs. Arnaud was telling Thomas in a low voice. "Your jacket's no longer in the trunk of your car. I took it out this morning. When no one was around, I took it down to the basement and got rid of it."

"Thanks, mother," Thomas said.

"Be careful about Rosemary," Mrs. Arnaud added in a near whisper. "You'll have to double your watch on her. At dawn I saw her heading off toward the forest. She must have gone back along the road, and God knows what she might have discovered!"

"She'd never be able to guess the truth," said Thomas in a reassuring voice.

"In any case, she'll do everything she can to discover it. Do you know where the peonies she picked came from?"

"I suppose from the bushes behind the outbuildings."

"You examined the bouquet even less closely than Rosemary did," Mrs. Arnaud said dryly. "Our peonies are of the *Moutan* variety, with woody stems. Rosemary brought in the vulgar peonies of China, which have green stems and which are at this moment blooming in every garden in Fontainebleau *except* ours."

Thomas sounded alert. "What does that mean?"

"That she went out to question someone. Maybe the forest ranger. You told me you'd passed there last night."

"The house was empty."

"What makes you so sure?"

"If the ranger had been there last night, he would have come out. There were cars passing, the shots...."

"Then why would Rosemary have hidden from us the fact that she went for a walk in the woods? I find it rather troubling."

"I do, too," agreed Thomas. "Especially since lying isn't part of her nature. She's normally the most direct person I've ever met. I hope she hasn't begun to lie to us."

"I believe it's worse than that," murmured his mother.

"What do you mean?"

"She was in a detective film...."

"So?" But Thomas answered himself. Suddenly he exclaimed, "Right! You mean that because she's acting in a police story, she might suddenly fancy herself as a private eye!"

"That's exactly what I mean. I think she's carrying out her own investigation and that, if she traces certain effects to their proper causes, she'll discover all by herself everything you're trying to hide from her."

Rosemary had heard enough. They were talking about her—again—as if she were some sort of annoying child, a bit precocious perhaps, but a child. She dashed upstairs, grabbed Mrs. Arnaud's pills from her cabinet, then ran back down again, even more quickly. Head high, she swept into the dining room.

Sitting at her place again, Rosemary found that it was impossible to swallow the smallest mouthful of food. She took the coffeepot instead and poured herself a large cup.

She was gripped by a desire to tell Thomas—and his mother—what she knew. But she held back. She still wanted to know what was going on, but it must be the truth. What would he do if he knew how far she'd progressed with her amateur sleuthing? At the moment Rosemary did not care to find out.

"You're very quiet, Rosemary. Thinking?" Thomas asked. There seemed to be a dangerous edge to his pleasant manner.

"Yes," she replied, "yes, I'm thinking about my business."

"The bookstore," responded Thomas. With heavy irony he asked her, "I'll bet that this week you haven't sold a single copy of my books, right?"

"At the start of the holidays, you can't expect...."

He interrupted with a burst of laughter. "Thomas Arnaud doesn't have many readers. Admit it!" Without waiting for her to answer, he continued in a confidential voice. "Don't worry. Happily enough, I have sources of income other than my royalties from dry old history books. What books do sell well in your store? Novels?"

"Detective stories, for one."

"Is that your favorite kind of literature?"

"There *are* some very good ones," Rosemary said defiantly.

He picked up an orange and started to peel it. A little ironic glimmer danced in the depths of his eyes. He spoke in a light tone. "I wonder if I shouldn't change genres myself and write a historical detective story. I'd be assured of at least one reader. Let's see, what could it be about? Do you have any ideas?"

The mocking expression on his face bothered Rosemary, but not enough to put her off track. She responded with an insinuating lilt in her voice. "A good subject and a good title: *The Memoirs of a Gentleman Thief.*"

"I believe that's been done," chuckled Thomas. His penetrating gaze seemed to be judging her, finding her foolish. She had a painful sensation of defeat. He was toying with her!

She heard the muffled ring of the telephone. Then Alice opened the door of the room. "It's for you, Mr. Thomas," she said. "I've switched the call to your office."

When he was gone, Rosemary excused herself. In confusion she hurried through the house, looking for somewhere to be alone, to think. One place came to mind: the gatekeeper's lodge, or cottage, which she had shared with her mother through the years of her childhood. She would go there to be alone.

She left the house and ran quickly across the lawn. The old lodge stood a few hundred yards from the main house. It, too, was built of ancient gray stone, carefully fitted and mortared. The slate roof slanted very low over the one-story structure and ivy climbed wildly over it everywhere. The gardener had to trim the vines every year so that they would not cover the deep-set, lead-paned windows.

Rosemary noticed that the flower beds were carefully tended. The irises stood out in tall profusion everywhere. Little rows of sweet alyssum tossed their heady scent into the air and marigolds made dots of flame. The borders hummed pleasantly with the bees that busied themselves there, and birds twittered drowsily.

Rosemary felt a choking sadness. She had not stood there for such a long time. A river of memories seemed to flow over her. Images crowded her mind, as vivid as yesterday: her mother, deeply absorbed in the flower beds, poking about with a trowel; Rosemary herself, as a schoolgirl in a blue tunic and brimmed hat, standing arm in arm with her mother, posing for a snapshot on this very doorstep.

"Mother," she said very softly. Mother, who smiled but seldom laughed. The highlights of her hair were as golden as Rosemary's own. She moved quietly through the long days before her last illness, when she could barely emerge from the house.

Rosemary fought back the tears. She was drawn, as if in a golden dream, to the doorstep. Her hand reached automatically behind the pot on the sill, and there she found the iron doorkey, still in the place where it had always been kept.

The key was placed in the lock as if by another hand; it turned and the heavy door swung slowly open.

The interior was dim in contrast to the shining day outside. Shafts of yellow light slanted in, dancing with specks of dust, and touching on the sturdy, dignified country furniture. Here and there was a gleam of burnished oak, or a splash of color on the print slipcovers.

Rosemary stepped inside, closing the door behind her. She stood in the silence—she had stepped directly into her own past.

"Rosemary, let me do your hair," her mother's voice seemed to say. "Here, help me with this seam; I'm getting dinner on—don't go tearing out again." The ordinary, familiar words seemed very clear, as if they'd been spoken only a moment before.

Rosemary looked around as her eyes became used to the dimness. She ran a finger over a table top; there was a light layer of dust everywhere—on the shelves, the glass lampshades, the arms of the rocking chair.

But it wasn't heavy dust, not six-year-old dust. The Arnauds had left the lodge almost exactly as it had been on the day Rosemary had left to go to live on her own. They had even tended the place regularly. Were they expecting her to fail, to come back here?

"They've always been very kind," she seemed to hear her mother say. "It's wonderful to be able to depend on someone—on the kindness of friends."

But kindness had not saved her mother, had not stopped her from being sad. It had not erased the long-ago heartbreak that shadowed their days.

Her mother had spoken of him sometimes, the man who had gone away. "Your father was a good man...in some ways," she would say. "You must remember that. He was weak and foolish, and crazy with money."

"Did he lie to you, mama?" Rosemary had asked in her young, small voice.

Her mother had smiled and hugged her. "Yes," she sighed, "he lied. But I can't help thinking he didn't mean it—that he'll come back to us—"

But he had not come back. Rosemary cringed as she thought of the pitying looks of the neighbors, of the icy perfection of Mrs. Arnaud, safe in her marriage and home. She had never said a word of disapproval to Rosemary's mother, but for years Rosemary had sensed it. How could she help comparing her own sensible marriage to mother's hasty and disastrous alliance with that irresponsible man? She must have felt impatiently superior to Rosemary's mother—with her vague gestures, her hair that flew away no matter how she tried to tame it, and her gentle, imprecise speech.

Sitting in the rocking chair, Rosemary dreamily lifted a worn album of photographs from the shelf beside her. The pages turned, small puffs of dust exploding from them.

There, neatly mounted on dull black, was a fading record of her mother's years. Short years, Rosemary realized, as her sadness deepened.

On the first few pages were old photos of family outings—a great country house, cars with wire spokes in their wheels, wicker baby carriages, dogs. There were young men in boater hats—Uncle this and Cousin so-and-so, Rosemary's mother had told her. They were all unfamiliar, these Laurins—the members of her mother's family. Rosemary had never met any of them.

Rosemary felt a familiar anger at this family who had totally rejected her mother when she married against their wishes. There they were, frozen in time, as remote and stiff-necked as she had always imagined them to be. She felt no connection, no kinship with them, wherever they were.

They had, she knew, provided her mother with some kind of meager allowance. But that was all. How cruel these ties of so-called honor were!

But her mother had never spoken harshly of them. "Perhaps they were right," was all she would say.

And here was a photo of grandmama, all coiffured and formal, sternly eyeing the camera. Rosemary's grandmother looked exactly like someone from another century, as the man at lunch, Ben, had said. How right he was! Even now, her expression had a glint of steel in it. She had set her heart against her only daughter—her only child—for reasons of silly pride.

Rosemary flipped the page angrily. What good were people like this, people without feelings? Grandmama had died when Rosemary was very young indeed. She felt pleased to relegate the woman to the past where she belonged.

The little history took a jump forward. Here was Rosemary's mother—not "mother" yet, but Arlene Laurin, a laughing young woman, pretty in a dress that the wind had billowed up above her knees. Arlene was on the arm of a man, dark haired, not terribly tall, whose smile was open and engaging.

This was Rosemary's father, Maurice Bally. This was the heartless man who had taken all he could from Rosemary's mother, then left her. He had left Rosemary, too, without a second thought or a worry in the world—except for himself. Rosemary had only the faintest memories of him—of a laughing man who gave her bear hugs, of the smell of tobacco and extravagant hair tonic.

How could her mother have clung to these photos—these memories—for so many years? But those memories were all she had, it seemed. The face in the photograph was indistinct, shadowed by sun. It might have been *any* man, Rosemary thought. But the charm was there, somehow, the charm that had drawn her mother and held her a prisoner for life.

Rosemary stared at the smile. It was something she had done many times before, when she was growing up. She had tried for years to decipher its meaning, this smile. Had he already known, even then, that he would break the heart of the woman who clung so trustingly to his arm?

Resentment welled up again inside her. If she could only find him someday, just once, to say exactly what she thought of him! When she was a teenager, she'd once asked Thomas to help her. They would trace him, would hunt him down. She would tell him in words he would never forget just what he had done!

Thomas has assured her that several efforts had been made to find the man. He even wrote several new letters. But the trail has been cold. Maurice Bally had apparently covered his tracks very well.

There were rumors, Thomas had said. People of the district had seen him in Normandy, in the south of France...he was using another name...he had married again—bigamously, for there had been no divorce...he had not married, but taken off to South America.

In the end Rosemary had given up. Evidently her father did not wish to be found. She had resolved, with Thomas's approval, to let the past lie.

And that, she thought now, *is what I should do today.* The book of photographs, full of her mother's memories, should be put away. There was the present to think about—a present that was filled with new, bewildering dangers.

She left the small house, closing the door on its memories and its enveloping sadness.

It was up to her to find out what was going on. Why had Thomas lied about the car? Where was the bloody jacket? And the gun?

Mrs. Arnaud had told Thomas to double his watch on Rosemary. She must be very careful from now on. They were playing some sinister game. They'd find out that she could be very clever, too!

As Rosemary crossed the lawn, she noticed that heavy storm clouds were gathering in the sky. They seemed to brood low over the tress of the forest, which stirred restlessly in a new, high wind.

The clouds were certainly appropriate, Rosemary thought. They perfectly symbolized her growing fear as she found, again and again, evidence of terrible secrets hidden at Clermont. The omnious sky echoed her foreboding.

They were watching carefully. If she continued to play detective, they were sure to realize how close she was to the truth. Would they try to stop her? Rosemary shuddered. Whatever happened, she must know the truth.

From the cottage she circled around to the back of the main house, passing beneath the kitchen windows, which were still open wide, in spite of the approaching rain. She paused for a moment, brushing back the hair blown into her eyes by a little gust of wind.

She heard Thomas's voice from inside. He was questioning Alice!

"I can't understand it," he was saying. "She hasn't been here?"

"No," Alice replied. "I've not seen her since breakfast."

"I wonder what she's up to? She can't have gone off into the forest again...."

Rosemary thought quickly. She could elude him—she must. Very softly she stepped past the window, and around to a doorway that led past the pantry to a back staircase. If she could slip into the house and on upstairs, Thomas would be none the wiser.

Reaching the door, she pressed her palm flat against the unyielding wood. Her stomach fluttered. It must not be locked! *It must open.* She tried the latch very gently. It would not budge. Steeling her body in determination, she gave the handle a very hard turn. Abruptly it yielded and the catch slipped open with a sharp click.

Had they heard? She drew a deep breath and stood motionless as she strained to hear any further sound. The seconds dragged by, but she could hear nothing from within the house.

Cautiously, silently, she opened the door. The hallway was dim and windowless, leading from this old entrance to the housekeepers' staircase. Once it would have been used frequently by servants who came and went without disturbing the family. It was very narrow and wound sharply upward. Moving softly in her espadrilles, Rosemary stepped in and closed the door gently. Then, with every nerve tingling, she walked silently to the staircase, passing Alice's pantry swiftly. She still could hear no voices. Thomas must have gone off somewhere else to look for her.

She congratulated herself for remembering this staircase, now little used. No one would be likely to think of looking for her here—and since she would not be seen going up the main staircase, it would be assumed that she was not upstairs at all.

It would give her time to explore, to look through the upper rooms—but for what? Rosemary realized that Thomas was probably far too clever to leave incriminating objects, whatever they might be, lying about. But she knew the house well. Anything new to its collection of art and furniture would be likely to catch her eye immediately. Anything as precious as the Sèvres ewer, which Thomas had flaunted, would indicate that the Arnauds were acquiring things beyond their visible means.

Perhaps I'll find the gun, she thought, almost unwillingly. If she could find the gun, she would have something with which to confront Thomas. Something he could not possibly evade or deny.

The staircase was very dark, despite the fact that it was barely noon. Tensely Rosemary felt her way up the steps, one at a time. It was difficult to gauge the distance from each one to the next, and several times she missed. Her feet made tiny thumps, and she prayed silently that no one would hear. The wooden steps were solidly built and creaked only the barest amount under her weight.

Her fingers brushed the walls lightly, touching the invisible surface, as she tried to judge the sharp turns before she came to them.

She gave a sudden start as her exploring hands encountered the silken, ghostly threads of a large cobweb. With her heart beating in panic, she tried to shake off the clinging web. She gasped as the torn threads moved like whiskers across her face. Choking back a cry, she brushed frantically at her cheeks and mouth. She rubbed her shaking hands on her jeans, trying to get rid of the web, and at last the thing was gone.

Heedless now, she scrambled quickly up the remaining steps, blind in the dark, reaching forward to touch the door she knew must be at the top.

Abruptly her fingers encountered the flat wooden surface of the closed door. Rapidly her hands sped over the surface, lightly trembling, searching for the knob.

It must be here, on the right—no, a little lower. Agonizing seconds passed as she fought to control her panic, her fear of this dark, stifling place. Then she touched it, the slightly cool, solid metal of the doorknob.

Seizing it with both hands, she turned it and the door opened onto the subdued light of the upstairs hall.

There was no sound, only a deep, expectant hush, as the old house seemed to await her next move.

Rosemary stood for a moment, composing herself, trying to settle the riotous beating of her heart. Then she walked toward the first bedroom to her right, her footfalls completely muffled by the thick carpet.

This was Mrs. Arnaud's room, which she had never willingly entered, even as a child. She felt like a thief as she silently turned the knob, swung the door cautiously open, and slipped inside. Every instinct within her rebelled at this intrusion, but the woman's words echoed in her mind. "You'd better be careful of Rosemary...she'll find out exactly what you're trying to hide."

If there was guilt, surely it belonged to the mistress of Clermont, who was privy to whatever secrets were hidden there.

Hastily Rosemary surveyed the room with its pale, imposing draperies that dimmed the daylight and the graceful lines of bed, dresser, wall mirrors. There were photographs in silver frames on the mantel: Thomas, Mr. Arnaud, even Rosemary and her mother.

That was odd, Rosemary thought. But the Arnauds were old friends of her mother's, good friends.

Again the absurdity, the upside-down terror of her suspicions struck her. Here in the pearly elegance of a lady's chamber, one did not think of robberies, of murder.

You've imagined the whole thing. The words mocked her. Rosemary was again filled with doubt. She must get out—this room could tell her nothing. A sense of shame filled her and she backed uncertainly into the hall.

I can't go on with this, she thought. It would be better never to know what was going on. She really didn't want to know! But another voice, from deeper in her consciousness, spoke. *She must know!* What was behind the cold facade that Thomas had created for himself? Why had he lied to her? Why had they all lied?

She forced herself to go on. The room where Thomas slept was the next logical place—perhaps she would find something there.

The room was comfortable and spacious. There were books everywhere with markers poking out of them. The wardrobe, dressers and tables were all made of whorled and classically carved walnut. There were brass humidors and cut glass decanters, plus a very fine stereo system with elaborately technical dials and a large selection of records, most of them classical, many of them experimental and rather difficult.

Rosemary was a little surprised. Thomas never talked much about music, but he was obviously a

sophisticated connoisseur. It was another bewildering face of this complex man whose life had once
seemed so bland and conservative to her. She shook
her head in puzzlement.

Her eyes fell on a closed oaken case, brass hinged,
that sat on one of the tables. She was magnetized
by it. It drew her across the room. Forgetful of her
self-consciousness at intruding upon Thomas's private quarters, she reached out to open it.

"I wouldn't do that if I were you."

The icy words stabbed through Rosemary and
she whirled around.

Mrs. Arnaud stood in the doorway. The ironic
smile on her lips did not reach her eyes. "Thomas is a
private sort of man. I don't think he'd like it if he
knew you were inspecting his personal belongings."

Chapter 8

Rosemary was rocked by an agony of shame. She felt a feverish blush spread through her cheeks. She struggled desperately for words. "I—I wasn't, really...I just thought...."

Mrs. Arnaud gestured impatiently. "I'm sure I don't know what you're up to, dear. You haven't been yourself at all since you got back. With all the mysterious nonsense last night and that knock on the head, you're becoming a stranger to us." She looked hastily around the room.

She must be wondering how long I have been here, what I might have found. Rosemary regained some of her composure. "I'm sorry. I didn't mean to intrude. I was just—looking for something—something I misplaced." The words were lame and unconvincing.

Mrs. Arnaud seemed to smile with more sincerity. "Well, whatever it is, you won't find it here. Why don't you come downstairs and we'll discuss what you'll do this afternoon."

Rosemary went willingly. She was off the hook for the moment—Mrs. Arnaud seemed satisfied merely to distract her, and unwilling to pursue the question of Rosemary's guilty foray into the private chamber.

"Thomas has been hunting high and low for you. He's *very* concerned," said Mrs. Arnaud, briskly escorting her along the hallway. "Why don't you go and find him? I've got a few things to do before lunch, and then we'll all talk."

Rosemary felt that the words were less an encouragement than an order. "All right," she agreed, feeling very awkward.

"Good. Now go downstairs, like a good girl. I'll see you shortly." Mrs. Arnaud withdrew into her own room and pointedly closed the door.

Rosemary stood silently for a moment, feeling overwhelmingly foolish. She had been caught in the act, and the older woman's assurance was her silent victory. Mrs. Arnaud had obviously reasoned that Rosemary would be too cowed by her embarrassment to cause any further trouble!

But that was not quite true. She was standing outside the library now, and instead of going downstairs, she walked into the book-lined room.

Rosemary closed the door of the library behind her. Thomas wouldn't think of looking for her here in this austere room, dedicated as it was to work and meditation.

Rows of shelves made from dark oak ran from the library floor to its ceiling. A large Oriental rug, woven in shimmering colors, lent a bright note to the somber atmosphere. Several chairs upholstered in leather and a long table laden with magazines completed the decor.

Rosemary noticed a pile of booklets covered with Thomas's fine handwriting. She wondered if reading these documents would in any way shed light on the man's secret life, but ambivalence swept over her and she refrained from glancing at them. To cut off the temptation, she sat down in the armchair farthest from the table where the manuscripts were stacked.

The smell of leather that filled the air struck chords in Rosemary's memory. When she had visited Clermont as an adolescent, Mrs. Arnaud would warn her that Thomas was working in the library and shouldn't be disturbed. She would come into the silent room on tiptoe and obediently sit down and watch as Thomas bent over his books. Deep in his work, he would pay her little attention.

Rosemary compared that old, familiar Thomas with this new one, with Thomas today. She recalled his faraway expression during breakfast, and she felt almost sick with apprehension. She wondered if she hadn't discovered too much. Perhaps the "other" Thomas—this alien, rather frightening and forceful Thomas—has always been there.

After all, what did she know of his emotional life? He had not always been this distant, this cool. But in recent years he had placed his inner feeling behind a wall of reserve. Beneath it she now sensed this explosive quality, this powerful arrogance.

But was Thomas capable of robbery, of murder? These were the compelling questions. The growing certainty of the answers filled her with fear. In her mind, she lined up the facts about Thomas that seemed to dovetail with the notion of him as a criminal. First, he had an unknown source of income. Second, he was virtually an expert on art and antiques. Third, he was a man who knew the area intimately and who was above suspicion. And most damaging of all, he seemed to have been involved in a mysterious, violent death, and to have covered up that fact.

Together, the facts made a clear picture to Rosemary. Yet she was unwilling to believe the worst. Without confronting Thomas, she must find a way to the truth.

The pile of booklets. She must look at them in spite of her scruples. With her heart in her mouth, Rosemary moved to the table where they lay. Trembling, she picked one up, then opened it. In Thomas's neat hand, she read:

The climb to the fourth story took all the strength and agility he possessed. With powerful arms, he pulled himself from window ledge to window ledge. At last he gained his objective. The knife glittered in the dark as he slipped it between window and frame, forcing it open. In one swift motion he was inside. Count Reynard had arrived!

Rosemary stared. *Count Reynard?* Here, in this library? Hastily, she scanned all the notebooks. They formed chapters. Chapters of a novel about a lone thief, about Count Reynard.

She tried to absorb this new jolt. Thomas seemed, beyond a doubt, to be the author of the best-selling book that formed the basis for the screenplay being filmed by Yves. And which contained all sorts of detailed lore on the burglary profession—especially as it applied to the Fontaine-bleau region!

It occurred to her that it would be just like Thomas—an arrogant game, pulling crimes and then writing books about them. A game of cat and mouse. It all fitted. She had always said that the author of the Reynard book seemed to know too much for his own good. She had been correct!

For a moment she was overcome by a new despair. Then, as if in a dream, she heard Thomas call her name. Without thinking, she rushed to one of the windows, opened it and called, "Here! Here I am!"

He turned around in surprise. Seeing her, he quickly headed toward the house.

Leaning on the sill, she watched his approach. She studied his features, trying to guess what feelings they hid.

"If you're looking for a detective story, you won't find one on the shelves in that room," he called. "I've been looking for you everywhere, wondering where the devil you were hiding."

"Come up here," she said.

With an acrobatic leap he jumped up toward her, grabbed the base of the balcony with his hands and, without apparent effort, pulled himself up to the ledge. He then hoisted himself to the balustrade and effortlessly swung over it. It was easy now to imagine him climbing drainpipes to attic windows.

He was almost as supple and agile as he'd been several years before, when he'd taught her gymnastics. One more item for the list of things proving his guilt, she reflected ruefully. It had become so clear. There was really no avoiding it.

It was equally clear that her knowledge would remain hers alone—she couldn't turn him in, no matter what he had done. But she must warn him, tell him what she knew. Then he might find ways to explain his behavior to the authorities who were sure to close in on him.

"Thomas," she began, faltering a little as his eyes held hers. "There isn't much time. I want to tell you that being *careful* is important...you'd better be careful."

"What? Leaping that balcony?" He laughed. "Rosemary, you're getting wrought up over nothing. You're imagining dangers and disasters again. It's *you* who should be careful!"

To Rosemary, the words carried a blunt threat. She was meddling in his affairs! She knew too much. And she *had* better be careful from now on. She dropped her gaze from his magnetic eyes.

"I've been looking all over for you this morning," Thomas said in a low voice, as he cupped his hand under her chin and raised her face to his once more. "Are you playing the shy coquette with me?" he teased.

Rosemary felt her legs grow weak with the confusion that was coursing through her. "N-no, of course not," she stammered.

"Well, right now I have something urgent to take

care of, but when I finish it, I want to spend some time with you," he ordered. "Don't disappear this time." He released her suddenly and, turning on his heel, strode forcefully out of the room.

Rosemary, awash in a welter of emotions, leaned against the centuries-old stone wall of the house, as if seeking peace and strength from its very substance. *Clermont*. It was a magnificent home, an almost understandable motive for crime. Thomas would do almost anything to keep the estate, she was certain.

She could smell the sweet honeysuckle and the dampness of moss on stone. How easy it would be to slip into the timelessness of this country life, to forget about violence and murder and dream through the days....

It was terribly ironic. She had expected Clermont to be a sanctuary, a respite from the rough-and-tumble, alien world of the movie nomads. But here she was, more dangerously close to violence and terror than she'd ever thought possible. Clermont's spacious gardens and parkland lay spread before her. Instead of peacefulness, their stillness seemed to be a breathless waiting....

A sense of urgency interrupted her reverie. Perhaps she should confront Thomas after all—warn him that his recklessness had given him away, that she knew more than he thought. If only there were some proof, something with which to threaten him, so that he would stop his dangerous games.

The manuscript? But it was hardly proof, damaging as it was. Rosemary stepped back into the library. The booklets lay where she'd left them. She decided to read the story through. Perhaps there was some sort of answer there.

Deeply immersed in the adventures of Count Reynard, Rosemary hardly noticed the passage of time. The tale was obviously a sequel to the one Yves was filming.

She thought with sudden clarity about Yves and the film unit. They would be wondering where she was. She had been so unnerved by the events of last night that she'd forgotten about calling them. She supposed that, in her absence, Lola would be forced to perform her own action sequences.

Lola was an ambitious star, chosen for the role of the lady spy who was Count Reynard's love interest because of her spectacular looks. In a curious way, she did resemble Rosemary. Their bodies were slender, their coloring golden, with tawny skin that tanned well. But the indolent Lola was more suited to erotic scenes, with which the film was rampant, than to athletic exploits.

Rosemary blushed. She had a quick mental picture of Thomas writing about the Count's amorous adventures. Staid, conservative Thomas! And with whom, she wondered, had he conducted his research?

Yves was more suited to the role of a Casanova. Among his Viking ancestors, she was sure there must have been at least one Oriental pasha. A harem of women seemed to surround him constantly, even on the remote film set. And how Lola resented the attention Yves paid to Rosemary! Placatingly, he would call Lola his Venus, comparing her to Rosemary, who was likened to the goddess

Diana. In private, however, Yves was casual about Lola. "I have to make her feel important. She's temperamental, remember. But it's you who are my Venus, Rosemary...."

Rosemary had noticed that during the day-to-day grind of filming, when scenes had to be shot over and over again, Yves's temper often frayed. No one could possibly keep up with his demands to get the film made as quickly as possible. No one was exempt from his rages at these times—not Lola, not the most experienced members of the crew—except Rosemary. His sunny manner had never faltered with her. And after a tantrum he was always so charming that everyone happily forgave him.

Rosemary was interrupted by Alice, who poked her head around the library door. "Miss Rosemary, there's a call for you. A man."

Rosemary hurried down the hall to a bedroom extension.

"Sweetheart!" exclaimed Yves's voice. "I've been so worried. Why haven't you called?"

"Yves, I've been terribly preoccupied. Something's happened. I couldn't make it to the set."

"Oh, forget that. Darling, what's wrong? What's happened? Look, I'll come over and get you...."

"*No!*" Rosemary blurted.

"But I must see you right away! You don't know how worried I've been."

"I'll meet you...in town."

"Okay. I'll take you to dinner, and you can tell me all about it. We'll go to Barbizon. It's a little more peaceful. Six o'clock—the garden at Le Relais. You'll be there?"

"Yes, definitely."

"And Rosemary...I've got something to tell *you*." His voice was tender. "Remember that."

Rosemary let the phone drop into its cradle. It rang again, immediately, with a shrillness that made Rosemary jump. Yves must have forgotten something. She picked up the receiver. "Hello?"

A man's voice, so loud that she had to hold the receiver away from her ear, spoke. "Hello. Is Thomas Arnaud there?" His tone was imperative.

Cautiously Rosemary replied, "No, not at the moment. He's busy. May I help you?"

"I'm sorry, but what I have to say to Thomas is strictly confidential. Would you please call him to the phone?"

"I told you, that's not possible. Then, on an impulse she said, "This is Mrs. Arnaud speaking. Is what you have to tell him urgent?"

"Very. It's of the utmost importance to him."

"I suppose it's about that business last night," Rosemary said, taking a shot in the dark.

"Exactly. You're in on this as well?"

"Yes, I am. Naturally. What's new?"

"Can you get in touch with Thomas?" asked the stranger.

"I'm going to try."

"Okay, then. I'm calling from Barbizon. Tell him that the man is dead. Before dying, however, he talked. And what he said is of great interest to the police. Do you understand, Mrs. Arnaud? Thomas is going to have to make arrangements for...."

Rosemary wasn't listening. Automatically she hung up the phone. Her mouth was dry and she had to lean back against the wall. She felt as if she had suddenly found herself in the eye of a tornado that was carrying her far away from sanity and reality.

The telephone call was a final confirmation of her suspicions. Incredible as it seemed, Thomas really was mixed up in the murder. The man on the phone must have been his confederate.

Rosemary suddenly felt as though she'd been kicked in the stomach. She'd hung up too quickly! She had found out nothing—not the identity of the dead man, nor the connection between the burglary ring and the death.

She ran quickly downstairs. She must find out if Thomas was in the house. He was indeed, and he stood at the foot of the staircase, staring up at her. He must have found out that she'd intercepted the phone call! She tried desperately to think of something to say.

"Where are you going in such a hurry?" Thomas demanded.

"Just—just to see a friend in town."

"Oh? And do you mind my asking who?"

"I most certainly do mind!"

The telephone rang again. The accomplice, trying to complete his message! Rosemary felt prickles of fear.

"Thomas? Telephone!" called Mrs. Arnaud from the study.

Thomas frowned. "I'll have to take that. Please wait until I get back. I want to discuss this further." He strode across to the study door and was gone.

Rosemary's heart was hammering. She had to

get out of the house now, before he found out that she'd intercepted his call. Scooping up her bag from the hall table, she hurried toward the front door.

But a sharp voice behind her stopped her in her tracks. "Rosemary, where are you rushing off to in such a hurry?" Once again Mrs. Arnaud seemed to have caught her in a guilty act.

Rosemary turned, her cheeks flaming. Thomas had sent his mother to keep watch while he handled the telephone call, and now she was trapped!

She stared defiantly at Mrs. Arnaud while she tried to think of something, some excuse that would get her out of the house. Her skull seemed to tighten with a throbbing echo of yesterday's headache. Her mind was whirling, but nothing surfaced.

She opened her mouth to speak, but no words came. Then her heart sank. Thomas had returned.

His eyes bored into hers. She seemed to grow suddenly weak and her knees trembled. Her throat constricted as she waited for him to speak, to tell her that he'd discovered her deception, that he knew she'd tricked his confederate over the telephone. Fear, deep and powerful, more overwhelming even than the horror she'd felt on the dark forest road, gripped her and held her fast.

"Rosemary, we've got to settle something right now. Come with me."

Pale with shock, she followed him meekly. Whatever was going to happen to her now, she had no strength to prevent.

Thomas strode purposefully into the salon.

Rosemary followed, robotlike, expecting her legs to betray her.

"Please sit down," Thomas commanded, turning once again to lock his eyes with hers. Wordlessly she obeyed, perching rigidly on the edge of her chair. Mrs. Arnaud was watching her intently. Rosemary felt like a small forest animal, trapped by two predators who would not toy with her before moving in for the kill.

If only she'd phoned the police! Why had she let them stall her? And why, when she'd had the chance this morning at the ranger's house, had she tried to divert the woman's suspicions? She'd actually been *protecting* Thomas! Old instinct, the solidarity of friendship and ties to people who were almost family—these had seemed to be the explanation for her behavior then.

Now, looking at Thomas as he stood in front of her, his jaw rock-hard and his eyes smouldering with a slow fury, she knew there was another explanation for her actions. With stunning certainty the idea fell into place and locked immovably.

She was in love with him. *She loved Thomas*— deeply, strongly, perhaps inevitably. Her rising fears of him, and *for* him, had made that clear. A new despair swept through her.

Then Rosemary became calmer and sat up very straight. She would face it, whatever happened now.

Suddenly she realized that her hosts were waiting for a response from her. Lost in her own thoughts, she hadn't heard anything that they had been saying.

"Excuse me, what were you saying?"

Mrs. Arnaud shook her head with a pitying air. "These movie people have really changed you, Rosemary. You never used to daydream like this. With you walking around in the clouds all the time, and a son who lives with Napoleon, I'm in good company!"

She affected a playful tone of voice, but Rosemary wasn't fooled. A certain tension was making the atmosphere heavy.

"...I was saying," continued Mrs. Arnaud, "that you ought to take advantage of this magnificent weather to have a change of scene. Take the car and go off together on an outing. Didn't you tell me once, Rosemary, that you've never seen the châteaus of the Loire? Thomas will take you to some of them, won't you, Thomas?"

"That's an excellent idea," he agreed, with exaggerated warmth in his voice.

What kind of a game were they playing? A few moments before, Thomas had spoken to a man, his accomplice in a murder, and had undoubtedly discovered that she'd intercepted the previous call. Mrs. Arnaud had then caught her trying to run away, trying to escape from the house. And now they were acting just as if it were any normal Sunday afternoon—as if nothing in the world were wrong!

Then the answer came to her. They were trying to keep her occupied, to get her away from Clermont so that she could find no more evidence. She would play their game, would pretend to go along with them.

Rosemary thought quickly. "On Sunday the roads will be swarming with tourists," she objected. "And I have to get back to the location tonight."

"You can leave tomorrow," cut in Mrs. Arnaud. "And Thomas knows some back roads in the Loire valley that are always quiet, even on Sunday. I'll see you later, children," she finished decisively. She left the room, carefully closing the door behind her.

Thomas sat watching Rosemary.

She wondered what thoughts lay behind that mask. He knew everything and was pretending otherwise! But of course he was too clever to admit anything to her.

She sighed inwardly. He need not worry. She had become totally lost, torn by the realization of her love for him. She was powerless to hurt him. Whatever he wanted her to do, she would do.

His voice cut into her thoughts.

"Where are you?" he asked bluntly. "In your bookstore or still out filming with the crew?"

She looked him straight in the eye. "Not for a single moment since I arrived here have I thought about Yves or about the film crew."

That was not the truth. But small lies paled in significance next to the deception that overlay everything in Thomas's life. She should tell him not to be a fool. She should rail at him, full of angry righteousness.

But she felt none of these things. She had no strength to confront him. She was conscious of just one thing—this new knowledge of hers, this certainty that Thomas was the only man she had ever loved or ever could love.

And that love was strangling within her, tortured by the knowledge of his guilt. She felt it as a physical presence—as a sharp and wounding pain.

The silence in the room was heavy. She roused herself. "Well, if you really want to go off on a country joyride, I suppose I'd better get ready."

Thomas seemed not to notice the bitterness in her voice. "Good," he exclaimed. "You do that! It won't really be so bad, you'll see. Come, now. Hurry and get ready."

She didn't see how he could carry on so. Each word was a cruel blow to her, hammering home his deceit, his cunning role playing. Slowly, she rose from her chair. "All right, Thomas," she said quietly. "If this is how you want things to be, I'll go along with it."

"I knew you'd agree. Nothing like a day in the country to take your mind off things." His smile was sudden, dazzling, and Rosemary again felt a pang go through her.

Slowly she climbed the stairs. On the landing she stopped to stare moodily out of the window. This morning's clouds, once so threatening, had blown away, leaving only a few shining white puffs against the summer sky.

The joyous day was a cruel counterpoint to the feelings that she carried heavily inside her. The hopeless discovery of her love brought her no joy, only an agonizing fear.

She could never tell Thomas, never let him know. Anyway, he would probably feel little if she *did* tell him. He could not care for her, ever, not this violent stranger with the name Thomas.

Sadly she wished for the old days, when he'd been like a brother to her—before he'd decided to use his fine mind and strong body in the service of criminal gain. Before he'd become a liar, a cheat, a killer.

Rosemary took her time having a shower. Then, in no hurry to go downstairs, she walked around her room in her bathrobe. She found it ridiculous that Thomas had picked up on his mother's idea that they go out for a drive. It was strange behavior for him, even if it was only a ploy.

And why the châteaus of the Loire? Thomas hated crowds, and she didn't like them much, either. At each stop they would have to line up in one of the Sunday battalions, which, guided by a commando, invaded the rooms of the historic châteaus.

From the window Rosemary noticed Thomas getting his car out of the garage. She saw that he had changed his old riding outfit for an almost too-formal combination: an iron-gray suit, blue shirt, and polka-dot tie with matching handkerchief. She deduced that lunch in a deluxe restaurant was going to be part of the agenda. She gave a tired sigh. It promised to be a thoroughly charming charade, this afternoon excursion.

Her sense of confusion at events had not destroyed the germ of rebellion in her. She slipped into blue jeans, the polo shirt and the espadrilles she had worn during her walk in the forest. Then she covered her head with a chiffon scarf. They would not go to a four-star restaurant, but rather to some modest inn.

She was about to close the window of her room when she noticed Mrs. Arnaud and Alice, both dressed in somber suits, hats and gloves, walking toward the garage. The two women were obviously going to church.

Because of the distance, Rosemary couldn't hear the dialogue between mother and son, but from Thomas's gestures she understood that he was advising Mrs. Arnaud of the latest developments. How could the woman go calmly off to church? The hypocrisy of the whole business struck Rosemary anew.

Why *should* she go meekly along with whatever course Thomas decreed? He was only getting himself deeper and deeper into trouble! How long did he hope to fool the police? Their net was closing tight. Yesterday they'd appeared at the film set—and they were scouring the highways....

She suddenly stood up very straight. There must be something she could do. She must not let herself sink into helplessness and despair. She thought feverishly. She would not, could not, turn Thomas over to the authorities. There was only one more course of action possible.

She must save him, must help him to escape from the authorities, to get away somewhere to a new life. She must help him in spite of himself.

She would have to resort to trickery, but she could save him.

She *must* save him.

Chapter 9

An unknown force now drew Rosemary outside of herself. She no longer trembled, and in her fevered yet lucid brain, the ideas formed and arranged themselves with orderly precision.

Mentally she traced the broad outlines of a difficult, yet realizable plan—they would escape the country, get away to Switzerland! Before evening they would be able to reach the border. She had little money on her, but she had brought her checkbook and an international credit card with her, so their material worries were temporarily resolved. She didn't have to think about everyday details—the first objective was to get the guilty person as far from Fontainebleau as possible.

Since Thomas was ready to take to the road, getting him to change direction would be relatively easy. What would be less easy would be to get him where she wanted to go without arousing his suspicions. Not until evening, when they were safely out of the country and all danger was past, would she reveal to him the truth. If she spoke earlier, she knew he would refuse to bring her into the adventure.

A line of anxiety again appeared between her eyebrows. The hardest thing would be to stop Thomas from using his blue car, the description of which might already be spreading across France. *He'll never agree not to use his car*, she thought, *unless. . . .*

She had a crazy plan that just might work. She would have to use every resource at her command. She would match Thomas, move for move, in the deadly game he had chosen to play!

She frantically pulled off her sports clothes and put on her dressy red outfit and matching shoes. Rapidly she checked the contents of her purse. Her papers were in order.

She ran back downstairs and out the door. Thomas had driven his car to Clermont's gates and stopped there. She had time to get her car out of the garage and drive it to the front steps of the house.

Thomas left his own car parked along the avenue and came toward the house with a nonchalant step. He stopped abruptly, however, when he noticed that Rosemary was waiting for him at the wheel of her little red car. As she had obviously decided not to leave her seat, he came up to her.

"What does this mean?" he asked, raising his eyebrows.

"It's simple. We'll take my car." She smiled brightly.

He smiled back. "Is this another one of your jokes?"

"I've never been so serious, Thomas. Today I just can't get into your car."

He looked bewildered. "But why?"

"It should be obvious without my having to furnish an explanation."

He scratched his head, his eyes perplexed and an amused smile on his lips. "You'll have to forgive me," he said, "I'm probably an idiot, but I don't understand."

She got out of the car, slammed the door and leaned against the body with the affected grace of a model presenting a new dress. "You still don't see?" she asked with a pout that she hoped was suitably coquettish.

He gave her a long, admiring look. "I see a very lovely woman who's dressed ravishingly." He'd never complimented her this way before. He was playing his game to the hilt!

"And the outfit I'm wearing doesn't shock you?" she asked.

"I must confess," said Thomas, "that I'd prefer a less aggressive red."

"But it's the exact color of my car!" she cried. "Is that deliberate?"

"What do you mean, deliberate? What are you trying to say?"

Rosemary was beginning to despair about convincing him to use her car. They had no time to waste!

Thomas seemed enormously amused. His sparkling eyes moved leisurely over her figure, slid to the hood of the little car, and then returned to her face. His arrogance was infuriating!

"I mean was it by design that you arranged the color of your dress to match your car?"

"Of course it's intended!"

"Outrageous!" he grinned. "What frivolity for a serious businesswoman. The container must be the same color as the contained. I never would have imagined it!

"But now that you've made me admire your sense of the artistic, you can separate yourself from the wrapping. The background that I offer you has the sure advantage of being bigger and more comfortable."

"It would offend my sense of the aesthetic," she retorted, smiling mischievously.

"Then we don't have the same tastes. I find the lines of my car much more elegant than those of your little buggy."

She flared up. "But haven't you understood? It's really a question of color!"

"Don't you like blue?"

He was ready to pick a fight. She controlled her temper and threw in a last argument. "I don't see how, dressed in red, I could possibly sit in a blue car with a white interior. I'd look like a Bastille Day parade."

Thomas's laugh quieted the flock of birds that was chirping in the trees above their heads. "Good Lord!" he exclaimed, "You're serious. How can you argue over such a trivial point?" There was a sparkle of pleasure in his eyes. He was enjoying the game!

Rosemary assumed a coaxing voice. "Please, Thomas, let's take my car. I'd feel ridiculous in yours, and all my pleasure in being with you would be ruined."

"Thanks for the thought, Rosemary," he replied ironically.

Had her teasing gone too far? There was a strange look in his eyes.

Without appearing to notice her impatience, he quickly reached out and took off the scarf that covered her blond hair. "If you go and change your dress," he suggested, "don't you think that would resolve the problem?"

She pretended to be confused. "You're going to think I'm silly if I cry," she said. "But I think I'm going to. I heard my horoscope on the radio earlier."

"So?" asked Thomas.

"Today the color red is supposed to be very important to us Leos."

He hesitated between indignation and laughter. Then, disarmed, he chuckled again and capitulated. Turning to the car, he gallantly opened the passenger door. "You win," he announced. "It would amuse me to drive your little car."

But instead of following him, she quickly opened the other door and sat down once again behind the wheel. "I'm the driver," she announced in a voice that left little room for argument.

She knew that he hated to be driven, especially by a woman. Seeing him lower his eyebrows and remain standing, she leaned forward and pulled at the bottom of his jacket. "Get in, Thomas," she begged, "and leave your pride in your pocket. I want you to judge how good a driver I am. I don't do badly, but I'd like to have the opinion of an ace driver like yourself."

He let out a groan that passed for agreement. After several seconds of hesitation, which to Rosemary seemed to last a century, he announced that he should park his own car and close the gates of Clermont. "Go and park on the avenue," he directed.

She sighed with relief and drove into the avenue. Because she knew that Thomas wouldn't allow more than one error on her part to revise the decision he had made unwillingly anyway, she decided to concentrate on driving faultlessly. She started the motor smoothly, changing speeds without grinding the gears.

Unfortunately, all the parking spaces along the roadside were occupied. While Thomas moved his car, she had to remain double-parked. Then she moved into the space he had left vacant.

She was just about to correct the wide angle between the sidewalk and her front wheels when suddenly in her rearview mirror she discovered a green sedan double-parked about twenty yards behind her. Inside the car was a man who seemed to be watching her.

Situated right on the edge of the forest, the avenue was bordered on only one side by the luxurious properties surrounded by thickly wooded grounds. The sedan was stopped at the end of the wall that enclosed Clermont.

Rosemary was certain that its occupant was waiting for Thomas and, in her nervousness, she stalled the motor. Her eye fixed on the enemy, she waited to see what the man would do as Thomas came out of the gates. She wanted to run toward Thomas, to stop him from coming out onto the street, but she could only sit immobile, her heart pounding and her mouth dry with fear.

Thomas left the property, closed the gates behind him, then calmly crossed the road toward Rosemary.

Nothing happened.

"Interesting parking job," he commented once he had seated himself next to her in the passenger seat and had tried to arrange his long legs as comfortably as possible. "If all drivers were as lax about parking as you and Favier, it would be impossible to drive down the street."

"Who...who is Favier?"

Fastening his seatbelt, Thomas made a vague gesture behind him. "The fellow in the green sedan. One of my old schoolmates. In grade school he was kind of a dope. Since then he's succeeded in real estate and has bought himself the loveliest house in the area.

"But I've never seen him park anywhere except in a no-parking zone or at a pedestrian crosswalk. Or else, of course, he double parks. Isn't there any way to push back this damned seat? My knees are up to my chin."

Slowly she emerged from her state of fear. "I...I don't know," she stammered. "There must be a lever somewhere. Why don't you look in the owner's manual?"

Because Thomas continued to complain about her "damned sardine can," she released in a rush all the anxiety she had accumulated during the last several minutes. "Oh, come on, Thomas, stop it," she cried. "My car isn't as solid as yours, I agree, but for once why can't you let yourself be driven without making a fuss? You won't die, you know."

She started the engine. As the car was still in gear, the engine sputtered and the car leaped forward.

Thomas turned toward her with a huge grin on his face. "I'm not going to die? I'm not so sure!" Then in a suave voice he added, "What did your horoscope say about car trips?"

Seeing her put on her blinker, Thomas protested, "Keep to the right, Rosemary. Good Lord! Don't change lanes!"

Ahead of them an approaching car was passing, and it grew larger with bewildering speed.

"The road has three lanes, so I have the right to use the center one, don't I?"

She managed to pull back between a truck and the bumper of a van. Behind her a concert of horns broke out, and either to warn her or to chastise her, the vehicles which approached flashed their lights at her. Her nerves must be very bad. She seldom made errors like this! But the game was to play dumb.

Thomas wiped his forehead while Rosemary asked, "How far have we come since Fontainebleau?"

"Four or five miles, and I'm starting to wonder how." Then in a more energetic voice, he added, "This demonstration had been sufficient. Pull over and let me drive."

She turned a deaf ear to the outrageous suggestion. However, knowing the risk she'd taken she drove patiently in the string of moving cars.

Eventually the traffic cleared a little, and Rosemary, without paying any attention to the speed limit, stepped on the accelerator again.

They approached a curve, which she took too quickly. With a screech of tires the car skidded to one side in much the same way as a skier would accomplish a slalom. Rosemary felt her beautiful assurance leaving her, but she managed to hold firmly onto the steering wheel.

The car finally regained its balance.

Thomas's voice rose sarcastically. "If you insist on continuing this random death course it's up to you, but I'd like to point out that your tank is on empty. You'd do better to slow down. The next service station is more than a mile from here, but at the speed you're going, you'll probably pass it without even seeing it."

She reduced her speed. The fact that she'd nearly had an accident brought her to her senses. She understood that she was no longer mistress of her and Thomas's destiny. She was not even properly in control of her car. Crouched inside her like a hunted animal, anguish once against planted its claws in her chest.

In a flash of clarity she realized that the plan she had come up with was unrealistic. To believe that she was able to lead a man as resolute as Thomas, without his knowledge, to Switzerland involved a lot of wishful thinking. It was clear that at the next service station he would insist on taking over the driving. The trip to Dijon wouldn't pose any problem, but how could she make him continue on to the border?

Around a curve half a mile farther, as the road stretched unhindered far in front of them, Rosemary understood with a shock that she would not have that chance.

Gesturing with their arms, two policemen were stopping all the traffic and obliging certain cars to park on the roadside. A little farther on, with their antennas raised, a black sedan and a gray van were parked, while a detachment of soldiers, wearing helmets and carrying machine guns under their arms, barred the road.

A mist obscured Rosemary's thinking. Everything around her once again took on the character of unreality. She recognized the danger approaching them; it wasn't by chance. She knew—she had always known—that sooner or later Thomas would be caught. The gray army van, the antennas, the red beacon on top of the police car, the rolls of barbed wire and even the slow swing of the policemen's arms as they stopped approaching vehicles had all been minutely detailed in the last scene of Yves's film script. It was the setting for the final tragic note on which the movie ended. Once again, reality had taken on the eerie echoes of fiction. A cold vertigo of fear gripped Rosemary.

"They've got out the combat artillery," said Thomas in a loud voice. "That's the same trick the force always uses."

Approaching the roadblock, Rosemary gave in to panic and started to speak without realizing what she was saying. "No, no, not that!" Instead of slowing down, she accelerated, wanting against all logic to break through the barricade.

Thomas seemed to understand what Rosemary was going to do. Very precisely, without any gentleness, he kicked her foot from the accelerator. With one hand he pulled on the emergency brake, and with the other he turned the steering wheel toward the side of the road.

One of the policemen came up and touched his cap. "Identity check," he announced laconically.

Numbly, Rosemary watched Thomas get his papers out of his jacket pocket and hold them out to the policeman. The man rapidly glanced at the documents, but didn't give them back right away. Instead he leaned forward once again and asked Rosemary for her papers.

She picked up her purse, but her fingers trembled so much that it took several seconds before she managed to open it and extract the case that held her driver's license and identity card. Her ears were humming as if something were vibrating in her head.

The policeman examined each piece carefully. He had thick, undecipherable features. All at once he turned toward his colleague, who was standing a few feet away. "Hey, Mark, come look at this."

The other man approached and looked at the card that his comrade held out to him.

It was then that Thomas put his hand on Rosemary's. He had long, strong and expressive hands. But she was so upset that she barely saw it, and hardly felt the contact. Her body, like her spirit, no longer seemed to belong to her.

The policeman had to repeat the order he had given her. "Would you take off your sunglasses, miss?"

It was Thomas who took them off for her.

"Recognize her?" one policeman asked the other.

"I sure do! It's our young lady of last night."

He leaned his elbow heavily on the lowered window and, as he held the papers out to Thomas, added in a half-bantering voice, "She looks shaken up. I'd advise you to take the wheel."

Too weak to protest, Rosemary climbed over into the passenger's seat while Thomas walked around the car.

The soldiers opened the barricade to let them pass and Thomas drove without a word to the gas station. He stopped at the pumps.

From the start of the incident, his features had become a mask. At the same time, in control as always, he had kept his thoughts to himself. Still silent, he glanced sternly toward Rosemary.

With her eyes closed, Rosemary desperately forced herself to organize the thoughts and images that reeled in her mind. Feeling Thomas's eyes on her, she lifted her lids and asked in a flat voice, "Why were they using all those soldiers?"

He shook his head and, as he gestured toward the attendant who was approaching the car, said, "Ask him. He's probably better informed than I am."

She rolled down her window and waited until Thomas had ordered some gasoline before she asked, "Do you know why there's a police roadblock on the highway?"

"Sure do," said the man. "Before they set it up,

the cops came over and questioned me. They want to be sure that a certain blue car doesn't go through here. Earlier today some people who, like you, were held up at the barricade, told me that only a few cars are being kept back for a careful search. Trunk, luggage—nothing escapes the eyes of the police."

"What are they looking for?" insisted Rosemary. "Thieves?"

"The cops didn't tell me, but when the army moves in, it's not for small game."

Rosemary sank back woodenly against her seat. She told herself that the game wasn't over yet and that they still had a chance. Thomas had got out of the car, and while waiting for the tank to fill up he walked around the car, kicking each tire as he passed as if to check the pressure. The gesture seemed to Rosemary to be an excellent omen. Thomas wasn't a man to neglect the smallest detail. In the short distance he had driven since the road-block, he must have noticed that in spite of its lack of power the motor easily held sixty miles per hour on the highway. If they skipped lunch they would be able to reach the border by midafternoon.

If Thomas had escaped the vigilant eyes of the police, she told herself, it was probably because they had used her car. Thomas had probably shown them phony papers as well. But this warning had put him on his guard. It was clear that he now knew where his best interest lay. She was sure that the idea of escaping the country was anchored in his mind.

Before getting behind the wheel once again, Thomas pushed back the driver's seat as far as it would go. This made it even more sure in Rosemary's mind that he was getting ready to make a long drive. She gave him a knowing glance, to which he responded with a friendly and vaguely perplexed smile.

Five hundred yards farther they came across the entrance to a major highway to the east. Thomas passed it without even slowing down.

"That's crazy!" she protested. "We're not going to keep driving at fifty miles an hour!"

"You're right," he agreed, taking his foot off the accelerator. A car passed him, and then he suddenly turned to the right onto a small dirt road.

"Are you mad? We don't have a minute to waste. Do you hear me, Thomas?"

He seemed determined not to hear her. The car jolted along the road, bouncing in the hollow ruts, but he steered with a firm hand toward the shelter of a small wood. He halted the car with an angry jerk.

"All right. Suppose you explain to me just what you're up to. I think I've put up with enough nonsense for one day, don't you?" Thomas's voice was low and deliberate. His eyes permitted no lies—and no escape.

Rosemary's fear for him was stronger than her nervousness now. "Don't be crazy, Thomas! This is no time to talk! You've got to get away," she cried.

He managed to look amazed. "Away from what?"

"From the police! Thomas, I know all about it. And I can't let you get caught...."

He gripped her shoulders, his face darkened by anger. "What do you know all about? Tell me—and stop acting like a child!"

"Thomas—the robberies, the dead man...don't you think I can figure these things out? But I don't care....All I want is for you to get away." She burst into uncontrollable sobs.

Thomas released his grip on her. She fought to control the wracking sobbing. At last she looked at him, her eyes filled with pain.

He stared quietly. "So that's it. You've found out—I'm a thief...a murderer...."

"Thomas, I—it doesn't matter. Only, please, you must...."

Abruptly he threw the car into gear. "We're going home, Rosemary." He spun the car around and drove very fast, back the way they had come, back to Clermont.

Rosemary wept quietly, occasionally glancing at him beside her as he drove. His jaw was clenched tightly and his eyes seemed to flash with a cold danger.

At the house, he led her out of the car and inside.

"Now then," he said firmly. "You go upstairs and stay there. We've got to settle this once and for all. But there are a few things I have to take care of first. Do as I say."

Rosemary nodded numbly. He turned on his heel and went into the study.

She stood for a few seconds, unable to move, her mind shrouded as with a fog. Then suddenly the mist cleared and she knew she had to do something. She would get away, get help. *Yves!* She'd forgotten about her promise to meet him. He was her only hope—somehow he would be able to help, to tell her what to do. She hurried out and quietly closed the door behind her. She ran toward the garage, and moments later was coasting through the main gates in her little car.

Driving toward Barbizon in the slanting rays of the afternoon sun, Rosemary desperately tried to sort her thoughts. The pieces of the puzzle were fitting together, inexorably, but the answers filled her with dismay.

What should she do next? The thought of Yves came to mind—clever, confident Yves. She could rely on him to keep the matter a secret, and to help her decide what to do. Her burden seemed to lighten a little.

Once in Barbizon, she bought a newspaper. She had arrived too early to meet Yves, but she decided to wait for him in the informal courtyard of Le Relais. The restaurant was incongruous for chic Barbizon—it had a hearty, provincial air about it. In summer, people sat at outdoor tables under an arbor.

Rosemary sipped an aperitif and studied the newspaper. There was no mention of a shooting or accident last night in the forest. At least Thomas had been clever in covering his tracks!

It was nearly six. She looked up from her reading. Yves stood at the courtyard entrance, his golden head framed by a leafy trellis. He stared at her for a moment.

Even at such a distance, Rosemary seemed to feel the force of a strong emotion coming from him. He strode directly to her and stood looking down at her for a long moment, his eyes searching hers.

Nervously, Rosemary spoke. "Yves, I'm so sorry.

I just forgot to call. I've been through a terrible time, and...."

He didn't let her finish. He swept her up into his arms and held her tightly. "I've been so worried," he whispered.

Rosemary disengaged herself, embarrassed by the public display.

He smiled warmly, unperturbed. "Never mind, love, I'm here now. You'll be all right. I've found you again and I want to celebrate!"

"Yves, I have to talk to you."

"Well, come on then." He took her arm and sat her down. "What is it? What do you want to talk about?"

"I don't really know where to begin. The most dreadful things have happened and it's all so hard to believe."

"Here, drink this. Now begin at the beginning."

"I don't know where the beginning is. I can tell you that I know who wrote *Memoirs of a Gentleman Thief*. I can hardly believe it myself."

"Aha! A major mystery solved. And who did write the book?"

"A friend of mine, a good friend. I saw a manuscript in his study. I shouldn't have snooped, I suppose, but there it was: a sequel, featuring Count Reynard again."

"But that's marvelous! Imagine knowing a famous author! Why is that so terrible?" Yves grinned broadly.

"But you don't understand! He knows too much about the real robberies. There's something more going on—something dangerous. It involves a murder, Yves. I can't tell you any more."

New interest kindled in Yves's eyes. "You've been involved with all this?"

"Not me, not directly, at least, but I've seen things, Yves. A bloody body in the forest, someone watching from the shadows..."

Someone, she feared, *whose name was Thomas!*

"Do you know who these people were?"

She lied. "No. But I'm on the brink of finding out. I can't say more. Will you trust me, Yves? Will you help me, without asking any questions?"

Yves smiled at her. "Of course. But can't we work on full stomachs? Let's have dinner."

Rosemary was barely able to eat, but Yves ordered a rich meal and insisted on having a choice wine from the cellars of the inn.

"We've got something to celebrate, darling," he announced. He took her hand in both of his, and looked very deeply into her eyes. "When you left yesterday and didn't turn up this morning, I felt like I was flying on one wing. I missed you terribly, Rosemary."

She started to speak, but he held up one hand. "No, let me finish. I've come to an important decision. Nothing really matters to me but you, Rosemary. I want you for my wife."

Rosemary's stomach fluttered. "I don't know what to say, Yves."

Rosemary had spent just over two weeks with Yves and the film company. The terror of the last twenty-four hours had seemed to put her at a great distance from his world, and from the constant excitement of the moviemaking. Now, watching him, so animated and enthusiastic, she remembered again the first days after their meeting.

His dynamic good looks, so attractive to women, had made her cautious. She had held herself aloof from the swarm of beauties who fluttered around him wherever they went, and her coolness had increased his interest.

She was certain that women like Lola, who seemed to regard Yves as her personal property, knew more than she about how to attract and hold such a man. Yet, the less she tried, the more ardent he became. Perhaps, she reflected, it was the sheer novelty of the experience. Her reserve had been a challenge!

And now here he was, his roguish eyes glitteringly intense as he pressed her to marry him! She was a little taken aback, a little amazed.

Yves smiled radiantly. "I could have my pick of women, you know," he teased. "But it's you I want, Rosemary. We could make it together, right to the top."

"I can't run off just like that, Yves. I've got my business to think of—" she started protestingly.

He didn't let her finish. "You're just letting your middle-class conformism get the better of you," he said scornfully. "You're stuck with all the prejudices and snobbery...."

Rosemary flared angrily. "I'm not a snob! And I've suffered too much because of middle-class prejudices to ever hold them sacred. But I've got *values*, Yves, values that tell me to be careful of the idea that anyone can get something for nothing!"

Yves became soothing. "I'm just trying to make you see how limited your life has been, how much you've missed, out of preoccupation with work and with life in a small town. You have dreams, Rosemary—I know it. Underneath it all, you're fiery. You want excitement. Haven't you ever wanted reality to measure up to your dreams?"

Rosemary sighed. "Yves, I don't know. My dreams have become a nightmare, somehow. I've had enough excitement to last anyone a century."

"Just say yes! We'll do it right away. We can run off to Paris tonight, and first thing in the morning, we'll have a civil ceremony. What do you say?"

Rosemary hesitated.

"Of course," he continued, "if you want a church wedding, we can do that, too, later on."

Rosemary's mind raced. It was a crazy idea to get married, to run off like naughty children...but she imagined herself with Yves, safely far away from the nightmare that had descended upon Clermont. She would be able to forget about robbers and sinister voices on the telephone; about Mrs. Arnaud with her solid wall of reserve that protected her son's strange double life; about Thomas and the trouble he was in....

But that was not possible.

She looked at Yves, at his shining, eager eyes. "Yves, I can't do that. I've told you, there are things I must understand. Events have taken a crazy turn and I'm confused. Everything seems to be topsy-turvy, and I'm being dragged along by forces I can't control. I must solve the puzzle. I must find some answers."

At her words, a dark thundercloud seemed to pass through the sky blue of his eyes, and Yves sat silent for many minutes. Rosemary was uncomfortable, but she was certain; she had chosen a course from which she could not be deterred.

At last he said reluctantly, "Okay, then. Let's solve this mystery. What do you want me to do?"

"That's just it. I'm not sure. I need to find out who it was that died. Could we check the hospitals for an accident victim—a man who died last night or this morning?"

Yves looked startled. "Of course. Why not?" He summoned the waiter. "Let's get out of here first.

"We'll need a phone," he went on, when they were out on the street.

"Perhaps it might be better to make a couple of visits," Rosemary suggested. Yves did not seem to hear her. He was staring across the street. Rosemary's eyes followed his gaze, and she gave a sudden little gasp.

Thomas was walking, quite unconcernedly, along the other side of the street. His eyes were straight ahead, as if he had not seen them. He walked directly to his car, which was parked at the curb a few yards ahead of Yves's light blue sportscar.

Of course! The man on the telephone had called Thomas from Barbizon. Thomas was here to meet with his confederates.

Or had he followed her here?

Rosemary pulled at Yves's arm. "Get back! That man over there mustn't see us!" Yves didn't seem to understand. He stood unmoving.

Suddenly Rosemary had an idea—they would follow Thomas, find out where he was going, whom he met! She spoke quickly and decisively.

"Yves, come on. We've got to get to your car. "We're going to follow him."

"Him?" Yves asked. "What's he got to do with it?"

"I'm not sure. But he's up to his neck in it." There was no point in identifying Thomas. Yves knew as much as was necessary.

Yves hesitated, but only briefly, as his customary recklessness came to the fore. "All right! Now I'm as curious as you are. Let's go!" He grabbed her arm and they ran to the car.

Thomas had got into his sedan. Rosemary could see him silhouetted at the wheel. He turned in his seat, seeming to check traffic coming on behind him, then signaled and slowly pulled out.

They were several car lengths behind him and could easily slip into traffic unnoticed. Rosemary concentrated on keeping him in sight, while Yves drove smoothly, manipulating the low sportscar with deliberate skill.

Soon they were clear of the village traffic. No cars now traveled in the space between Thomas and themselves, so Yves held carefully back.

For several miles they drove in silence. Thomas was moving at a leisurely speed. *He feels perfectly safe*, Rosemary thought. She glanced at Yves, who stared ahead in concentration, seeming to share her tension.

Where were they going? And what would they find at the end of this journey? Rosemary almost regretted her decision to follow Thomas. She had an irrational sensation of falling, as if everything she knew and trusted, everything she valued, were being torn from under her.

But Yves was there, strong and confident at the wheel of this powerful car. Rosemary tried to relax. Dusk was falling rapidly and Yves switched on the car lights.

Suddenly, the taillight on Thomas's car began to flash. "He's turning," Rosemary murmured urgently.

"Right." Yves flicked on his blinker.

Ahead, Thomas turned off the highway onto a smaller road that led into the forest. Rosemary tried to orient herself, but she was unfamiliar with this part of the great wood. They would have to follow, hanging back as far as possible, and hope that Thomas didn't spot them.

Yves made the turn and Rosemary peered into the unmarked blackness ahead. There was no sign of Thomas's car. "Oh, hurry," she creid, and immediately covered her mouth. Her voice had been very loud in the grim silence. But Yves responded instantly. Rosemary was jarred violently to one side as they rounded a curve.

There it was! The red taillights of Thomas's car bobbed along in the darkness. The road wound through the trees. They were occasionally brushed by the reaching branches as they sped along. Thomas seemed to have picked up speed, confidently negotiating the dips and hairpin curves.

Yves's jaw was set; the muscles were carved by black shadows in the dashboard light. He seemed to be part of the mechanism of the car as he drove—a silent, efficient machine.

The car ahead slowed suddenly. Rosemary realized that they were approaching a familiar landmark—the rotary turnaround, with roads that radiate in all directions like the spokes of a wheel. Yves slowed the sportscar down, watching intently.

Ahead of them Thomas's car lights bounced violently. He was driving through the construction work that half blocked Devil's Detour!

A sickening sense of familiarity washed over Rosemary. She had been here before: was the nightmare to begin again?

Very slowly, Yves approached the rotary. Thomas's lights disappeared into the dark tunnel of the Detour.

Rosemary fought waves of panic. "Yves, I don't want to go any farther...."

"It's too late," said Yves tersely. He maneuvered the sportscar into the entrance to Devil's Detour.

He was traveling fast—too fast. The taillights of Thomas's car had disappeared. Yves's low-slung car jounced wildly as its tires bit into the sand and were bruised on the rocks. Rosemary expected that at any moment they would go crunching into the rocks by the roadside. She forgot her initial panic—the feeling was replaced by an alert tension.

She could see perspiration standing out on Yves's forehead as he fought the wheel. His face was knotted with the strain.

They surged up over a rise and the headlights caught something red. Thomas's taillights—they'd caught up to him!

But Rosemary instantly realized that the redness lacked the incandescent glow of burning lights. It was a reflection—as Yves's beams again picked up the red spots, she realized, too, that they were not moving.

"Stop, Yves. Stop now!" Rosemary breathed. Quickly he braked and switched off the lights.

Without thinking, Rosemary flung open the passenger door and scrambled out of the car. She was completely swallowed by darkness, unable for the moment to see anything. Blindly she hurried along the road, stumbling in the sandy ruts. She could hear little but the pounding of her heart. An expectant hush seemed to have fallen among the trees. She couldn't even hear Yves, though he must be following behind her.

She seemed to be wading in a void, through shadows, heedless of what she might find.

The sky was lighter than the blackness of the trees. She could see patches through the brooding limbs that linked themselves above her. Her senses began to tingle with an animal awareness. Gradually, silhouettes of tree trunks formed themselves; her eyes were becoming accustomed to the night.

Then she could see, just ahead, a blackness blacker than the rocks and trees, with gray patches here and there where metallic trim gave off a faint glow. It was the silent hulk of a car. It seemed to be tilted at a strange angle. The trunk was sprung wide...the driver's door was open....

This was not Thomas's car. It was here again, silent, spectral, unmistakable. Terror froze Rosemary in her tracks. It was a trick, a horrible joke, and Thomas was hiding somewhere, waiting to trap her!

Frantically, she turned to run back to the sportscar, back to Yves.

But with a jolt that set her head spinning, she was seized and held fast by arms that crushed her like steel bonds. A powerful hand slapped over her mouth and pulled her head back sharply.

In an agony of fear, Rosemary knew that the chase had ended.

Chapter 10

Rosemary's stomach churned. So this was where playing detective had got her—trapped and helpless on a dark road. She struggled, but one arm was twisted behind her back, held in an iron grip. Tears of pain welled in her eyes.

Thomas must have realized they were following and had waited here in ambush!

Where was Yves? Why didn't he help? The darkness! He couldn't see her! If she could only get free, get those viselike fingers from her face and call to him.

Twisting, she tried to lash out with her foot, but steely muscles wrenched her around again, preventing any movement.

For the second time in as many days, she feared desperately for her life.

Suddenly she was blinded. A powerful light shone directly into her eyes. The crushing arms tightened around her.

"All right, let her go," barked a strange male voice. She could see no one; the glaring flood of light made their surroundings even blacker.

Rosemary's heart pounded and her lungs were seared with pain as she struggled to breathe. A voice within her screamed, *Thomas, let me go! Don't make it worse!*

Suddenly someone stepped into the glare. His head and square shoulders were starkly outlined by the floodlight. The rest of him was deeply shadowed. Terrified, Rosemary tried to see his face.

The man spoke quietly, with a dangerous edge to his voice. "You heard. Let her go."

Abruptly Rosemary was shoved, flung headlong into the man's arms. At the same instant, she recognized the voice.

Thomas!

But who....? There was a sound of scuffling, running, curses. She turned quickly.

Yves stood in the angry white light, scowling at her. Someone had a good grip on him, someone in a beige raincoat.

"Yves? I don't understand...what's going on?" Thomas pressed her shoulders reassuringly.

Yves was spun around, forced against the car. There was a metallic click as handcuffs were snapped on, pinning his arms behind him.

He twisted around again, his face a mask of fury. "You don't understand? Well, ask *him!*" he spat. "*He* knows everything." The chords in Yves's neck stood out. "You're all a bunch of damned fools," he shouted.

"All right, Delorme. Take it easy," said the detective.

Yves stood up straight, his face twisted into a sardonic grin. "What's this prove anyway? All the cops and robbers, the melodramatic night scene? I had nothing to do with it!"

"You had plenty to do with it." The detective was the man with the pipe, from yesterday. "You proved it, Delorme, when you panicked. We thought you might."

"It proves nothing! You can't tie me in with this business."

"There's something you don't know about," said the detective. "The man you thought you killed didn't die right away. He told us an interesting story. All we needed was some confirmation from you, Delorme. You blew it, blew your act completely."

Yve's mouth curled in contempt. Squinting in the glare, he turned toward Rosemary and Thomas. Then his face melted into a strange parody of a smile, a bizarre echo of his old devastating charm. "This wasn't what I'd planned. Murder is so...clumsy, so lacking in finesse. I got angry. He shouldn't have meddled, shouldn't have made me angry! I didn't plan to shoot him, only to tell him I meant business. But he insisted, he wanted to back out. And all because of you, Rosemary. He wanted to *protect* you!"

Yves's laugh sent a chill through Rosemary. She found herself clinging to Thomas, wide-eyed and silent. Yves's face was a caricature of the overwhelming charm he had once used on Rosemary.

"You know, Rosemary, it wouldn't have been such an unpleasant fate for you. I was able to put a lot of authenticity into my lover-boy role. We might have had a pretty good time...." He looked suddenly like a sad little boy, dropping his head. "It would have been a first for me, I guess. You were different—not like all those other dumb females." He looked in her direction, his face painfully twisted against the glaring light. "But you love me, I know you do!" he shouted.

The detective shook him roughly. "That's enough, Delorme. You'd better take it easy."

Yves was pulled toward the police car, stumbling and lurching as he strained to see Rosemary's expression. "You love me, Rosemary. Don't you?" His voice rose raggedly, desperately.

Rosemary did not respond.

He cried out, more loudly, as they shoved him into the car. "You do! You love me! Rosemary?" His shouts were cut off by the firm thud of the police car's door and the roar of its engine.

Rosemary's lips were still. Her mouth was dry, clamped shut; her skull seemed to press tightly on her brain. She was frozen very still, here in the dark shadows and screaming white light of the forest road. The dull pounding of her heart seemed to ebb and she was washed, at last, by the first gentle waves of relief.

Trembling, she turned and looked up at the somber face of the man who held her. His eyes, worried and intense, searched hers. "Thomas...?" Her voice sounded small and weak. Then she was seized with a strange elation. *Thomas was not a murderer.*

He held her very close, very tenderly. "I'll

explain," he said gently. "Come on. Come home."
Slowly they walked together.

More lights flooded the forest now. There were
more cars parked a few yards ahead on the road.

They got into Thomas's car. He settled her into
the passenger seat, wrapping his jacket around her
shoulders, then drove carefully along the winding
ruts of Devil's Detour toward Clermont.

Rosemary's thoughts spun and tumbled. Yves
had shot the man. Yves was guilty. But Thomas
had behaved so strangely! What did he have to do
with it? And *why* had Yves shot the man, whoever
he was? Who was the man? *He had been trying to protect
me. From what?*

"Thomas, who was the dead man? Why was he
trying to protect me?"

Thomas glanced at her. "I'm going to let him tell
you himself," he replied quietly.

"I'm so confused, I don't even know how to think.
You said he was dead!"

"Yes, he is." Thomas would say nothing more.

They were approaching Clermont now, by the
back gate. The stone wall loomed up before them—
the border of a sanctuary.

They were met at the door by Alice and Mrs.
Arnaud, whose stricken faces reflected Rosemary's
disheveled appearance.

"Get her a brandy," said Thomas. "She's had a
long night and I think it's going to be longer still."

Mrs. Arnaud stared in alarm at her son.

"It's all over now, mother. Rosemary deserves to
have some questions answered. Get her comfortable. I'll be back in a minute."

Still puzzled, Mrs. Arnaud watched Thomas stride through the hall to the study. "The salon, Alice," she said absently.

"I'm fine," Rosemary insisted, gently brushing aside Alice's motherly arm. "Yes, let's get settled. I'm determined to hear this through to the end. I want to know what's going on."

Alice bustled quickly to the sideboard and filled three brandy glasses. Then she left Rosemary and Mrs. Arnaud alone in the room.

They sat in silence. Mrs. Arnaud stared at the figured pattern of the carpet, her hands folded tightly on her lap. She seemed to be filled with some deep apprehension.

Then softly, she spoke. "I want you to know something, Rosemary. I think that what you are about to hear may shock you deeply. It may be a mistake for us to tell you now. But I am glad that you're to know at last, because...events...have forced it upon us."

Rosemary's throat tightened with foreboding at what was to come. She sensed that whatever it was would affect them all deeply: Thomas, Mrs. Arnaud, herself. The confusion of the last few days returned—could Thomas possibly be involved with the art burglaries after all? What was she going to be told—by a dead man? How could a dead man speak?

Thomas stood in the doorway of the salon. Rosemary and Mrs. Arnaud both turned toward him, their faces pale in the stillness of the lamplight.

Quietly he shut the door behind him. As he came

into the room, Rosemary noticed that he was carrying something, a small radio or tape recorder. Without speaking, he set the machine on a table and plugged it in.

He looked at Rosemary. His dark features were grave. She sat farther back in her chair. Perhaps, after all, she did *not* want to hear the answers to her questions....

He spoke. "Rosemary, there is really no way to prepare you for what you're going to hear on this tape recording. I think, however, that it explains itself. Please listen carefully. We'll answer any questions you may have afterward."

He pressed a button and, after a moment's distortion, Rosemary heard a man's voice.

"Rosemary, this is for you," it began.

There was something familiar about the voice. She tried to place it—someone near, someone recent....

"I've just about had it, they tell me," the voice went on, rather unevenly. "I'm not famous for good deeds...I've lived by my own rules, mostly. But I can't let this pass, and while I've got a breath left in me—as the saying goes—I'm doing my best to make a couple of things right for you.

"Rosemary, this is Ben, Ben Reay. I've been shot, as I probably deserved, by somebody whom you should not trust." There was a scratchy silence on the tape for a few seconds.

Ben? Ben, the character actor! Ben was the man Yves shot! Rosemary leaned forward, straining to hear every syllable.

"I should start at the beginning. First of all, my

name is not really Ben Reay. I am Maurice Bally. I'm your father. I left you years ago, I know, and I have done nothing better since. I've been less than perfect, I guess you'd say, but I *am* your father." Here there was a cough or two on the tape.

Rosemary realized that her hands were clenched and white as she stared at the machine. The room seemed to fade around her, and the only reality was the voice. Images of Ben came flashing to her—a gray-haired man, rather kind to her. *My father?* A rush of very old anger went through her. *My father—the deserter and con man.*

"You can't have anything but resentment for me, I know. But wait. It gets worse. For years I've been a professional gambler and fence. In case you don't know, that's a receiver of stolen goods. I've operated all over France, wherever the pickings were good. I never came back to Fontainebleau, though, not after I had walked out on your mother and you. I knew that you were basically cared for, believe it or not; I had good contacts here.

"I knew certain other things, too. It's a rather Victorian tale, but you're unaware of the will your grandmother made out—so I'll run over it for you.

"She was enraged when your mother married me because she suspected, rightly, that I might do what I *did* do—blow the wedding settlement and your mother's personal assets on gambling in the stock market. Once the money was gone I got bored. I'm not excusing it, just telling you. I cleaned out the bank account and took off. For the rest of her life, your grandmother refused to allow your mother any more money than was barely necessary. She was taken in by friends, the Arnaud family.

"Grandmother was very rich. When she died, she *still* didn't want your mother to get her hands on the money. She made up a very special clause in her will.

"*You*, Rosemary, and not your mother, were to inherit her estate. Grandmother liquidated her holdings and put all the cash in trust, collecting interest. It is, believe me, a tidy sum. The old lady, ever vigilant, added an extra twist. She wanted you to be safe from men like me.

"You were *not* to know about your inheritance until one of two things had happened. Once you were safely married, you could be told—right *after* the wedding, and not before. And, of course, your bridegroom would know you as yourself, not as a rich girl. Failing that, you should be told on your twenty-sixth birthday." The voice paused.

"Neither of those things have happened, but I feel that a dying man can reveal the facts to you. And as long as nobody tells the lawyers, you're okay. I don't give a damn. It's all foolish, and it left you open to terrible dangers.

"No one, by the way, was supposed to know the conditions of the will except the Arnauds, who are your trustees. But I bribed a law clerk when your grandmother died, a few years back. Simple greed motivated me. How, I wondered, could I get my hands on some of that money? I felt entitled to it. . . .

"Opportunity was slow in coming, but a few months ago, it knocked, loud and clear. I was in the south of France. In a gambling casino I met a very charming young man. Over drinks, he rattled on about his ambitions. In the way of rascals, we had pegged one another. He wanted to make big money as a movie director, he said. He had a property; he only needed financing. He was talking whimsically about robbing the casino.

"I had something eminently more practical in mind. He had mentioned that Fontainebleau would be his movie's locale. That brought to mind my interest in your inheritance. I had observed that my friend was a real killer with the ladies. Perhaps I could initiate a romance. If you, Rosemary, were married to a man of *my* choice, one who was beholden to me, then I'd have access to the family money.

"I told him of my plan—as much as he needed to know, at any rate. I also offered to help him out with funds for his film, in exchange for an ironclad agreement that I'd be paid many times over when he had married you.

"Things were hot for my organization in the south of France, anyway. It was a fine opportunity to do a little 'speculation' in art and antiques. I knew the area well. But that hasn't much to do with you. Suffice to say that I carried on illegal activities, which I've explained to the local police, while posing as an actor in the movie company. The director, whose name you've guessed, was my young friend. He struck up an acquaintance with you, successfully. He brought you along to work on the film so he could keep an eye on you.

"But something happened, something we hadn't

counted on at all. I got to know you a little bit, Rosemary. You were my own daughter, with your freckles, your green eyes, your mother's tawny hair. And you were open and honest and courageous. You didn't deserve Yves, I decided.

"I tried simply to tell him. 'The deal's off,' I said. He flew into a rage. The fellow's a megalomaniac! He wouldn't hear of it. He was absolutely determined and, I thought, maybe dangerous.

"There was something else I could do. I could get you away from him—warn the Arnauds to protect you. I phoned their estate, got hold of Thomas, the son. I told him who I was, to his shock, and asked him to meet me last night. The only place I could think of was an old road near the estate—Devil's Detour. I wanted to keep it quiet, just spill the story and let him take it from there. The burglaries didn't have to come into it."

The voice stopped again—there was rustling, another cough.

"I'm getting tired, Rosemary.... Anyway, I didn't reckon on Yves. He followed me into the woods, to that old road. Demanded to know what I was doing. I stupidly told him. There was quite an argument, and somehow, he shot me. Things went black. Next thing I knew, I was in this clinic.

"Thomas tells me he found me, with the car crashed into the rocks. Yves must have done that, trying to make it look like an accident. Who did he think he'd fool? But the damage wasn't bad; Thomas got me out, just drove the car, slightly dented, a few miles to the doctor's. He called the cops, but I was unconscious. There wasn't much they could do...about Yves. When I came around, the doctor told me I was in bad shape. The police had got hold of my record and were very curious. They were hovering over my bed with a tape machine. They were interested in the burglaries and in who shot me. I told them a few things...and I asked them afterward to let me talk to you, Rosemary. It's all been a damned waste, except maybe for this. Goodbye."

The tape swished, spun and clicked off.

There was a ghostly silence in the room. A dead man had spoken.

Chapter 11

Rosemary was completely numb. After several long moments she raised her eyes. Thomas stood watching her closely, his eyes filled with sadness and concern.

"When did he die?" she finally murmured.

"This morning."

"My father," Rosemary whispered. "I don't want to think about him now, Thomas. Someday I'll listen to the tape again, when I'm ready to try to understand."

She lapsed into silence.

When she spoke again her voice was flat and toneless. "So you wanted me to come here last night because my—father had phoned you...."

"Yes. He said Yves might be dangerous," replied Thomas.

Yves, Rosemary thought. He must have given that phony tip to the police. He wanted them to stop her, delay her, so he would have time to go after "Ben." "The shadowy figure in the woods. . . ." She halted.

"That was almost certainly Yves. He saw you, and he must have watched me as well when I managed to drive the car away. I had gone on foot to meet your father. The distance from the house was not very great," said Thomas. "Yves must have been frantic. What should he do? As soon as Ben was missed on the movie set there would be questions. He knew the police would trace the car, but it was registered in the south, under your father's real name, so they might not make an immediate connection. Your father had taken care to absent himself from the set when the detectives came by. Yves tried all the hospitals and the morgue, apparently, but he couldn't find your father, dead or alive. I had taken him to the clinic of a friend, near Barbizon."

Mrs. Arnaud spoke. "Dr. Benet couldn't come that evening to see you, Rosemary, because he was busy trying to save your father's life."

Thomas continued calmly. "The only thing Yves could do to get information was telephone you. When you were willing to see him, he decided he was safe for the time being."

"He must have thought so," Rosemary said, with some alarm. "He was pressing me to marrying him, right away!"

Thomas's eyes seemed to flicker. "And what did you say to that?"

Rosemary hesitated. "Do you know, I was actually tempted? I was so shaken by the violence, by the fact that you, Thomas, seemed to have a secret life as a thief, that you might have been involved in a death. And Yves was always so energetic, so compelling...."

Thomas interrupted. "He apparently had quite a hold over you for a while." His dark brows knitted in a frown. "Did you love him, Rosemary?" he asked in a low voice.

Was that a flush on Thomas's cheekbones? Rosemary couldn't be certain. "No, I don't believe I ever did. He was exciting, romantic, dangerous...."

"Just like Reynard the thief," grinned Thomas.

Rosemary suddenly thought of something. "The Sèvres ewer. Why did you tell me it was like a trophy to you?"

Thomas smiled broadly. "My remark certainly added a supportive element to the thesis you were forming, didn't it? The story's simple. I bought the piece for very little from a rather shady pawnbroker who didn't know its value. I was delighted to be able to turn the tables on him, because he'd cheated plenty of people in his day. That's all."

"And when you followed me to town...."

"I couldn't stop you from going to Yves, but I had to keep an eye on you."

"And then we followed you...."

"Well, that was part of the plan. We did want to lure him to the old road. I was in contact with the police up till the time you left the restaurant. We hoped he'd be unnerved by the duplicate 'scene of the crime' and say something damaging. It was harebrained—a spur of the moment thing. I relied on your sleuthing, your detective instinct, which you were using so well around here. I thought you might try to follow me. If you hadn't, the police would have closed in at some other spot."

"Why was there all the mystery last night, after I said I'd seen the car? Why did you try to convince me I hadn't?" asked Rosemary.

Thomas and his mother both looked apologetic. "It was a delaying tactic, Rosemary," said Thomas. "I didn't know what to tell you about your father, since what he'd said had been incomplete over the telephone. I wanted to try to speak to him, and asked the doctor to call if he regained consciousness. Mother knew where I was, and I let her know about the shooting. We didn't know the full story until after you'd left to meet Yves."

Rosemary realized that the sinister voice on the phone had been that of the doctor.

"Rosemary, rightly or wrongly, we wanted to keep you out of it until we knew. Of course, when the police said that Yves had been named the killer, I shot off to town after you. I let myself be seen openly, as you may have guessed. Perhaps, since Yves had seen me before, moving your father from the scene, he could be prompted to try to do something about me. He did—he followed me right into our trap."

Rosemary sat very still in her chair.

"Look, you can't absorb all this; it's too much for one night," Thomas began gently.

"I'm *not* finished." Out of the welter of questions that whirled in Rosemary's head, one seemed to surface insistently. "All right. I know about the bloody Windbreaker now, and the phone calls, and Thomas running around in the night." She stood up and stalked back and forth. "But there's one thing that still puzzles me a lot." She gave Thomas a piercing look. "If you're *not* a cat burglar...."

"And I know you thought I *was!*" Thomas said. There was a glint of amusement in his eyes.

"If you aren't, then why have you got secret manuscripts about Count Reynard right here in this house?"

Thomas raised his brows in wonder. "So you knew about that! Well, I wrote *The Gentleman Thief*, of course. But writing about him and being Count Reynard is hardly the same thing!"

"Well, why didn't you say you wrote the book?" Rosemary demanded.

"Because he's a snob," said Mrs. Arnaud suddenly. "He thinks he's above that sort of thing." She looked at him severely. "I think it's a wonderful book."

"I did it for the money," Thomas said defensively. "I used the background of real crimes around Fontainebleau and invented a crook to go with them. But I couldn't write under my own name. I'm a historian. People wouldn't take my real work seriously if they thought I wrote thrillers."

Mrs. Arnaud smiled. "You see, Clermont's been in trouble, financially, for a year or two. Thomas decided to scrape together the back taxes by writing a little potboiler. We didn't dream it would be a best-seller. Now he has a huge advance payment for a second Reynard book." She hesitated. "But I suppose the movie won't be made, after what's happened...."

"No doubt someone else will pick up the option," said Thomas. "We've got lots of money, anyway!"

"I'm rich, too," mused Rosemary. "No. I have to be

twenty-six or I have to be married. Whichever comes first."

Mrs. Arnaud rose from her chair. "I'm so terribly tired. I do hope you two will excuse me. It's been a long evening." She laid a gentle hand on Rosemary's arm for a moment, then left.

Thomas and Rosemary were alone in the salon, with the quiet night outside.

"Would you like to get some rest now?" Thomas asked. "You look very tired."

Rosemary stared at him for a long while. He returned her gaze steadily. Finally she spoke. "I know I look tired. I must be a fright, in fact!"

"No," he protested, "I didn't mean...."

"Thomas, there is one last question. Do you remember, out there in the darkness, after they took Yves away?"

His gaze faltered a little. "Yes."

"You held me very closely, Thomas."

"I was frightened for you. I had put you in danger."

"Thomas, I have something to say to you." She crossed the room and stood squarely in front of him. "I don't really care if I look a wreck, or if I've turned out to be a secret heiress, or if you're a famous thriller-writer. There's something more important."

Then the words would not come. She felt very small looking up at him, at his steady, calm eyes, which were like morning light, like a new world to her. Inwardly she trembled, losing her resolve. She must not speak to him. She didn't have the right, even now, to say....

"Rosemary, I love you." The words had tumbled out, had fallen into the silence between them. They could never be taken back.

Rosemary felt her cheeks burning. The hand she had pressed to her mouth, to stop herself from speaking, shook very slightly. There was an endless moment of silence while shadows seemed to drift, deep in the gray eyes that held her.

"You do?" Her lips moved very softly, as if in a dream. Then Rosemary was enveloped, folded tight in his arms. "You do!"

He held her against him, gently and surely. They stood together, clinging in the lamplight. Rosemary's world condensed to the warmth and strength of his embrace.

He drew back far enough to look into her eyes again. His fingers gently traced her throat, her chin, the corners of her mouth. "It's been so long," he whispered. "I've waited for you, Rosemary." His mouth touched hers, softly hesitant. Slowly, the kiss deepened until Rosemary felt herself drifting, growing light. His lips seemed to demand her soul.

At last he drew away. His eyes were glittering and tender. "I love you, Rosemary. I probably always have," he said, his voice husky with emotion. "I couldn't say so till now—"

"Oh, Thomas. Why not?"

"It wouldn't have been right, my little rebel. You had to seek your own life first."

"I always thought you didn't notice me at all!" protested Rosemary. "Except, of course, for bossing me around."

"Well, imagine a guy who's used to projecting a big brother image to a little tomboy, suddenly finding out he's putty in the hands of a certain green-eyed young lady! Of course I had to assert my superiority. Besides, there was that little matter of your inheritance. How would it have looked if an impoverished scholar had married the innocent heiress of whose fortune he was trustee?"

"You? A fortune hunter? Don't be silly." She settled her head comfortably on his chest.

"You thought I was a cat burglar, didn't you?"

She gave him a fierce look.

"No, Rosemary, I'm serious. There was no way I could express my feelings for you, as long as we were broke. You'd have been hurt, I'd have been hurt. But now I'm richer than you are, so I can happily press my suit!"

He kissed her again, on the eyelids, the tip of her chin, on the mouth.

Rosemary was aware of the first pale blue light of dawn glowing in the windows.

"From now on, my love, from now on," said Thomas, and she felt, quite possibly for the first time in her life, that she was at home.

SUN DRENCHED the morning streets of Fontaine-bleau, as the town sleepily set about the day's business. Shopkeepers were unrolling their awnings and setting out the obligatory pots of summer flowers. Splashes of color glinted on plate glass windows and seemed to dance on the bright pavement.

Rosemary clung tightly to Thomas's arm as they stood in front of The Reading Room.

"You see, Thomas. You're famous at last." She laughed as they admired the display. There, carefully arranged, were copies of all Thomas's books, his rather weighty volumes of Napoleonic history. They were neatly stacked beside a photograph of the author, who looked suitably tweedy and severe, posed with a pipe in one hand, the ever rebellious lock of hair somehow forced into place over the forehead.

"Don't you think I make a fine-looking scholar?" Thomas asked, tenderly squeezing Rosemary's arm.

"Well, it's really a little out of character, Monsieur Reynard. I think you ought to speak to your publisher about it," bantered Rosemary.

"This is my serious side, you've got to realize. I'm surprised to see my boring old books so prominently advertised."

"Bertha and I agreed that we should give our local authors a boost," Rosemary said, suppressing a smile. "But now we've *really* got something to promote, with you being the reality behind the mysterious count...."

Thomas was severe. "No, you don't. That's one dark secret I want to keep. And don't you tell Bertha, either."

Rosemary sighed. "I suppose it helps sales, this mysterious nom de plume." She kissed him lightly on the chin. "All right. My lips are sealed. But come on in. We've got to tell Bertha all the news!"

"If she doesn't know it by heart already," Thomas joked as she pulled him inside.

Bertha fairly bubbled with joy as they entered. "Rosemary! Thomas! It's so wonderful to see you together like this!" She hugged them both warmly. "It's been all over town for the past two days—the robbers rounded up, the crimes all solved, and that business in the woods. The newspaper didn't have it all, but I heard—"

Rosemary laid a hand on her arm. "Wait, Bertha! We've barely had time to recover! I've been sleeping around the clock, it seems—"

"And you look marvelous! That awful bruise is gone, and you're yourself again." Bertha paused breathlessly and gave Thomas a fond look. "And you're with Thomas Arnaud. You know, I always *thought* . . . ."

Thomas blushed and spoke hurriedly, "And how did you know about us? A hotline to Alice, I suppose?"

Bertha looked modest. "Nothing important ever happens around here without my knowledge." She smiled. "But that fellow Yves. I can't think why I didn't see through him."

"Nobody did," said Rosemary. "He was quite an operator. A charmer who'd worked at it for years."

"A bit of a psychotic, too," said Thomas shortly.

Bertha looked puzzled. "I'm still not clear on what he was up to. . . ."

"Well," Rosemary began hurriedly, "he had an involvement with the ring and I was—useful—to him. He decided to sweep me off my feet." Rosemary looked up at Thomas. Her voice sank as she went on. "I'm afraid he almost did. . . ."

"These swindlers! You never know who to trust these days. And *murder* . . . ."

"He had a falling-out with his robber friends and there was a shooting, so the police trapped them all. . . . It's completely bewildering, really."

Rosemary looked cautiously at Bertha. The part of the story about Maurice Bally had obviously not registered with her yet. Or had it?

Bertha returned her look. Her eyes became sad. "Rosemary, your father's name was in the newspaper. I'm really very sorry...I knew him a long time ago...he wasn't *all* bad."

"I know," Rosemary said. "I have to get used to the idea that he was even alive all those years. I never knew him, not the man he had become. I know that my mother loved him, and there must have been reasons for that. And I know that he did something for me in the end, something very important. I—I'll have to spend some time thinking about it all."

"But he was one of the burglars?"

"Yes, he was. He was the mastermind, so to speak." .

Bertha held her chin in both hands. "Oh, it's really so terrible. A man from the past, a stranger to you...he died before you knew him. Did you have any idea?"

"No. He worked, or pretended to work, on the film with us. But he was really funneling information to his confederates, who were raiding houses at night. Yves was sort of involved...I suppose it'll all take some unraveling still."

Bertha brightened. "Well, it's all for the best, I suppose. And now here you are, safe and happy!" She beamed at them both. "No one will wish you anything but happiness after all you've been through."

"Thank you, Bertha," said Thomas. "As a matter

of fact, my, ah, wife-to-be has a number of things to tell you."

Apprehension clouded Bertha's gaze. "Yes, of course. You'll be getting married. And I'm so happy for that! And you'll be giving up the business. It's really all right. I can work anywhere. Why, I'll march up to Courteau's gift shop and I'll convince them—"

"Bertha! Wait!" Rosemary laughed. "I've got a far better idea. You're too good to go to waste. I want you to take over completely, be my manager."

"Oh, I can't really do it without you!" Bertha cried, but pleasure seemed to swell within her and she smiled broadly.

"Oh, yes, you can," said Thomas firmly. "Rosemary will be busy, but you can hire whomever you need."

Rosemary chimed in excitedly. "Yes, and maybe we'll even expand. Buy out the flower shop next door, move in racks and racks of new books...."

Thomas gave her a fierce squeeze. "Hey! You're getting all wrapped up again. You're going to be my wife, remember? And as for the money...."

Rosemary's green eyes glowed. "Yes, Thomas, I'm going to be your wife. But while you're writing your books, sometimes I might be out selling them for you! It doesn't have to take up all my time. I'll be there for you always, I promise."

She turned again to Bertha. "There's no reason anymore to struggle for money. But this gives us a chance to really work The Reading Room into something we've always dreamed about. You'll have a free hand, without me hovering around. I know you'll do a good job."

Bertha became confident, energetic. "Oh, it's fantastic!" she crowed. "Listen, right now I've got an idea for a new window display...."

"No changing that window," glowered Thomas.

"But there's such a huge demand for this Count Reynard book! I thought I'd do something special— now that the case is broken, as they say."

"No cheap thrillers," declared Thomas with a mocking smile. "I want *my* important historical studies to get *some* attention. After all, I'm in a position of privilege with the boss!"

Rosemary gazed at him for a long, rapt moment. "Certainly," she said softly. "Whatever you say, darling."

He bent to kiss her, very lightly. Rosemary returned the kiss, then gently pushed him away.

"*But*," she laughed breathlessly, "we've got the public to think about. And they want to read Count Reynard's adventures. You're going to have to share the window!"

Thomas groaned in mock dismay. "What have I done? Come on, let's get out of here before you invent any new outrages!"

He swept her toward the door with one strong arm. "Goodbye, Bertha. Take care of things. I'm rushing this woman off to blissful serenity as mistress of Clermont. Don't call for at least a month."

Bertha folded her arms and smiled.

They stepped out into the sunny day. Rosemary felt sure and proud as she held Thomas's arm. His face was unclouded and confident, reflecting the brightness of the sun.

The terrors of the past few days dissolved from

her mind. Some of the wounds would heal slowly, she knew. But they would heal.

A gentle sensation of peace and security came over her. She rested her cheek lightly on the fabric of Thomas's sleeve. It was warm, rough textured and very real.

As Thomas looked down at her his gray eyes softened, and she knew that her world had at last come into focus. This gentle supporting arm was Rosemary's reality, her home.

She would never give it up.

"*Madame?*" he whispered as they stood beside his car. He bowed low and his eyes glinted with dangerous roguery. "Please enter my humble carriage." With a grace worthy of any gentleman thief, he swept open the door and helped her in.

They set off once again on the road to Clermont. This time, though, the road wound through a forest that was rich not with echoes of evil, but with the green promises of the future.

4 FREE

MYSTIQUE BOOKS
Your FREE gift includes . . .

Your FREE gift includes

House of Secrets—by Denise Noël
Proper Age for Love—by Claudette Jaunière
Island of Deceit—by Alix André
High Wind in Brittany—by Caroline Gayet

Mail this coupon today!